BEATS OF
THE PA'U

BEATS OF THE PA'U

Maria Samuela

TE HERENGA WAKA
UNIVERSITY PRESS

Te Herenga Waka University Press
Victoria University of Wellington
PO Box 600, Wellington
New Zealand
teherengawakapress.co.nz

Te Herenga Waka University Press
was formerly Victoria University Press

ISBN 9781776920037

A catalogue record is available from the
National Library of New Zealand

Published with the assistance of a grant from

ARTS COUNCIL OF NEW ZEALAND TOI AOTEAROA

Printed in Singapore by Markono Pte Ltd

for Tou, Steve and Harry

Contents

The Promotion

Kura stood on the doorstep barefoot and drunk, a brown paper bag tucked under his arm. He didn't recognise Taki at first, but the shape of his father's eyes looked familiar. Kura's slim build must have come from his mother's side. Taki had a pot belly and Kura's belly was flat and taut, his skin as dark as his outlook. Either the sun in Wellington had been blocked by skyscrapers that drew long shadows on the footpaths and roads, or Taki always dressed in too many layers, his skin shielded from natural light. Also, it was hard to be touched by the sun's rays when you spent your days toiling inside a concrete abattoir. So his father's complexion, which Kura had been told was once as rich in colour as the most fertile soil, had become sallow.

A grey Cortina with tinted windows was idling on the road behind them. Kura turned in time to see the car roll down the street, heard it beep twice. Then his father was coaxing him into the house, clicking the front door, sealing his fate.

'Kia orana, son.'

Kura flinched at the word 'son'. His father's wife, Tu, greeted him and pulled him into her arms, and he felt his body stiffening like the trunk of a coconut tree.

When he was a boy, he used to wrap himself around the tallest tree outside his grandparents' house, the rough edges scraping against the insides of his thighs as he climbed to its peak. At the top, he'd hook his ankles, hugging the trunk. His backside protruding, naked toes erect. He'd look down over the coastal village, searching beyond the horizon.

Tu introduced him to his younger brothers – Abe, Moses and Joseph. They mumbled hello and shook his hand with limp, awkward wrists. His sister Mere lifted baby Teresa to his face and he hesitated before holding her, keeping her wriggling body at arm's length. Her legs dangled uselessly in front of him, but eventually he softened at her gurgling and rested her tiny body against his chest, planted a clumsy kiss on her cheek. He felt her recoil at the whiff of beer on his breath, and he panicked and passed her back.

'Abe,' said Tu, 'go get your brother some socks. Clean socks.' Kura felt the heat rising in his face. He loathed the attention, and also it meant that his father's wife had noticed his bare feet. Possibly she thought he owned no shoes of his own, had none of the basic belongings her own children took for granted. He stared down at his feet. They were flat and wide and, though you couldn't tell by looking at them, his toes were turning numb.

Tu spoke to him in Cook Islands Māori, and when he responded he could tell by their raised eyebrows his siblings were impressed. He guessed they knew only English.

He let Tu lead him through the sitting room and into the dining room, where the table was set with the family's best crockery. He had noticed the gaps in the cabinet beside the fireplace, where ceramic plates were displayed like works of art. The other children in the family, he noticed, used the plates from the kitchen cupboards.

An extra chair, a stool covered in orange and cream vinyl that clashed with the others, had been slotted in around the dining table. Joseph sat on the stool while the rest of the family sat in what Kura thought must be their usual spots, eyeing up the space at the table that Kura now filled. Abe returned with a clean pair of rugby socks and the whole family watched as Kura slipped them on, his hands starting to tremble. He hadn't realised how cold his feet were until they were swaddled in the knitted wool.

The table was piled high with food – two roasted chickens and a small leg of lamb, two bowls of chop suey, two large mounds of mainese, slabs of taro and freshly made coconut sauce in an old bottle of Jim Beam, the empty bottle gifted to Taki, who prohibited alcohol in his house. Stacks of sliced bread and a brick of butter and two jugs of orange cordial bookended the food. Kura stared at his empty plate as if he could manifest some of that food upon it. When he looked up, his baby sister was gawking at him from her highchair. He envied her lack of knowing and her helplessness. Hers was the kind of helplessness that came from infancy, not from having landed in a foreign country alone.

Taki bowed his head and paused to let his family catch up. Without having to check that they had, he said, 'Let us pray.'

The family said grace as one voice, the words spilling from their mouths in a single spiel. The siblings recited the words between shared secret glances, peering over at their new brother, who kept his eyes on his plate.

After grace, hands flew across the table. Chicken thighs were torn from chicken breasts and chicken wings, the white meat sucked from wishbones to be pried apart later for empty dreams. The leg of lamb was hacked into thick chunks

of meat, the bone stripped clean of its flesh and presented
to Taki like a medieval mace. Mainese and chop suey were
heaped beside the meats, and everything was drowned in the
salted coconut sauce.

Tu grabbed Kura's plate and covered it with food. 'Eat
up, my boy. You're too skinny for round here. You need to
put on some weight or the wind will blow you away.'

He picked at a drumstick and mashed some of the taro
into the coconut sauce with his fingertips.

'Don't be shy,' said Tu. 'You treat this house like your
home.'

Kura's fingers skidded across his plate and drops of sauce
spilled onto the tablecloth. Before Kura had a chance to
even look up from the spillage, Tu had leapt from her side of
the table and sopped up the mess with a tea towel.

'Sorry,' he said.

She told him not to worry and to eat up before his food
got cold. Her smile wavered and he wondered how long
she'd known about him. If she was the same age as his father,
then something made her seem older. Her skin was clear and
wrinkle-free, except when her lips turned up at the edges
and the lines on the outer sides of her eyes became visible.
She wore her hair in a bun, and apart from the few strands
of grey at her temples, which you only saw if you were
standing right next to her, it was as black as he imagined
it was when she was only eighteen. Which is how old his
mother was when she died at his birth. It wasn't all those
things. Something else about her made her seem older than
he thought she might be.

'Mere,' Tu said to her eldest daughter, 'pour your brother
a drink. Don't just sit there.'

Mere grabbed the glass beside his plate and poured

cordial to the brim. They avoided each other's eyes and she returned to her plate quietly.

'So you can speak English,' Moses said. 'Or is "sorry" the only word you know?'

Tu clicked her tongue at her second-eldest son, who started to sulk.

Apart from the grace, their father hadn't said anything. Kura looked over at him, then back down at the tea towel soaking up the sauce on the tablecloth. He could feel his father's eyes on the side of his face.

'Do you go to church?' Taki asked.

Kura had seen only one photograph of his father. From his parents' wedding day, six months before the day he was born. He'd seen other pictures of his mother – two baby photos, one photo when she was a schoolgirl, and the family photo of the grandparents who brought him up and their thirteen offspring. But that wedding photo his grandmother kept between the pages of her Bible was all he knew of the man his mother married. Until Taki's letter arrived.

'No,' Kura said, shaking his head.

He felt Taki's disappointment. It seemed to float above the table like poison mist. 'Well,' he said, 'as long as you are under my roof, you will go to church with the rest of the family.'

His siblings sniggered. They stopped when their father fixed his gaze on them, giving each one of them the look.

*

Although it was cold, Taki was glad to be back on land. The voyage from Rarotonga to Auckland took twenty-six days and was far from restful. There were eight other islanders on that boat – all men, all young, all seeking a new life and home in a new land. They worked on that trip to help pay their fares, and to save on costs they rationed the taro and bananas they'd brought with them. Fish became their primary diet, so by the time they docked in Auckland's harbour – tired, cold and hungry – they were all desperate for some meat.

'I can't wait to get to my sister's place,' Taki gloated. His English was broken and limited but his optimism was in over-supply. He described the roast mutton and mashed potatoes she would serve him, the fresh peas plucked from her vegetable garden, the thick gravy flavoured with the meat's juices, and the cool, sweet orange cordial served in a glass, maybe with some ice cubes.

'That's what they eat in New Zealand,' he said. 'Then ice cream and fruit salad – then a cup of tea and cake.' At nineteen, he was one of the younger men in the group, but his unquiet manner made him seem older and more knowing.

He caught a taxi to the address in Papatoetoe. His sister's letter, which she'd written in the language of his mother tongue, was deeply creased. He'd memorised the words like a hymn. He twitched uncomfortably in his father's best suit. At least he looked good. He admired his reflection in the window, turning his head to the right, then left, then right again, smoothing back his dark wavy hair with the palms of his hands. He shifted nervously in his seat as the taxi approached the house.

His sister greeted him at the front door. 'Welcome, my brother,' she cried.

They were still hugging long after the taxi had left. For a brief moment Taki was again that skinny thirteen-year-old his sister had known back in 1950, before she'd fled the family home. Communication between her and the family had become sporadic over the years, but when she drew Taki into her home she knew to say nothing about the baby or the dead wife.

Her house was a palace compared to the two-roomed family homestead they'd left behind in Mauke. Family photos of herself, her Papa'a husband and their children decorated the sitting room walls. 'Eis made from polished shells and coloured plastic, cut and shaped into ever-vibrant frangipani blooms, hung like bunting over the Victorian-inspired wallpaper on the walls of the corridor.

The aroma of a home-cooked meal comforted him, distracted him, his mouth watering at the thought of his first roast mutton. His brother-in-law, patient and thoughtful, quieter than Taki had expected, offered him a beer but was unsurprised when Taki refused it. Instead, Taki watched his nieces and nephews play Last Card on the floor. They snuck a look at their new uncle, which he returned with a wink that made them blush and giggle.

'Aere mai kai manga,' his sister called from the kitchen.

The family seated themselves around the table. His sister said grace – thanking God for her brother's safe journey and asking Him to watch over Taki as he continued his travels south. Taki listened half-heartedly. He was more interested in the safe journey of the roast to the table. He watched his brother-in-law's every move as he delivered it across the room.

'I cooked this meal especially for you,' his sister said, beaming.

Taki stifled his disappointment as the platter of roasted fish and taro was placed on the table in front of him.

'Welcome to New Zealand, brother.'

*

After lunch, Abe showed Kura the bedroom they would share. The first thing Kura noticed was his brown paper bag. The small bundle of clothes that it carried was placed on top of the single set of drawers, his jandals on the floor beside it. Abe must've done that when he collected the socks. Or perhaps Tu had snuck out before to help make the bedroom more homely. Then he noticed the guitar resting in a corner. The six nylon strings were taut against its slender neck, the ends clipped neatly at the tuning pegs. He picked it up and ran his fingers over the fretboard, picking at the strings with his thumb.

'You play?'

Abe's voice startled him. 'No,' he lied. He put the guitar back against the wall and stood awkwardly beside it.

'Took me ages to save up for Mary,' said Abe. 'Lucky I could get extra shifts at the college.'

'Mary?'

'The guitar.' Abe picked it up, plucking the strings.

Kura didn't feel the need to press for more details. 'You work?' he asked.

'Part-time, after school, with Mum,' said Abe. 'Hard work, but the money's good.' He grinned. 'Any money's good, eh, when you're already skint. That's the best thing about starting at the bottom, brother. Only way is up.'

He handed the guitar back to Kura. It was your average guitar, the basic kind that even children could learn on. But to Kura it was the finest musical instrument he'd ever held. He sat down on one of the single beds and lay the body of the guitar flat across his lap, his hand over the headstock.

'That's my bed.'

Kura moved to the other bed and felt the springs creak beneath him. He sank into the edge of the mattress and worried his backside would leave an imprint. After a moment, he held the instrument up to Abe, like an offering. 'Play something for me,' he said.

'Nah, bro,' said Abe, waving his hands at him. 'You play something for me.'

Kura rested the body of the guitar against his stomach. He strummed a G chord and fiddled with the pegs until he was happy. He played A and then C, and once he was certain all the strings were tuned right, he plucked the notes to a song from home.

'You know this one, brother?' he asked Abe, not missing a beat.

Abe laughed. 'Teach me, bro.'

The song was making Kura homesick. He lost himself in the rhythm, like the gentle sway of his grandfather's fishing boat moored in the reef. He felt lulled back to his grandparents' house, the humble wooden homestead furnished with four queen beds in its front room. He remembered the sparsely concealed long drop and the open-fire cooker where their meals were prepared, both just footsteps from the house. The crowing roosters in the morning, the scent of blossoming gardenias. The warm rain tapping against the tin roof.

He started to sing and his words carried through the room. Abe seemed to be studying his fingers – the way they were crooked at the knuckles, the amount of pressure applied to the strings. Kura angled his body so Abe could see more clearly. He supposed the lyrics sounded like traffic to his brother, but he persisted. Surely he'd heard sounds like it before – at christenings and weddings and twenty-firsts.

'Dad says you have to shut up.'

They looked up. Moses was in the doorway.

'You have to keep the noise down,' he said to Kura. 'These walls are like paper. We can hear everything.'

Kura stopped playing. He got up and returned the guitar to the corner of the room and the springs in the bed creaked once more when he sat back down. Moses nodded and left. Kura stared at the doorway as the footsteps made their way down the corridor.

'Don't worry 'bout him,' said Abe. 'He just needs a girlfriend.' He grabbed the guitar and handed it back to Kura. 'When did you get here?'

Kura strummed the guitar, careful not to make too much noise. 'Yesterday.'

'Where did you stay?'

'With my mother's family.'

'Your English is good.'

Kura said nothing.

'Why didn't you come home? We could've picked you up from the airport.'

Kura shrugged.

'In Porirua? Your mother's family, I mean?'

'Yes.' Kura paused, then grinned. 'They had party for me.'

'Don't blame you then.'

More common ground, besides the guitar and their father. 'You like beer?' he asked Abe.

'Yeah, bro. Don't tell the old man.'

Abe showed Kura the empty drawers and the space in the wardrobe where he could hang his clothes. He didn't need much space; the clothes in the paper bag barely filled two hangers.

'That all you got?'

Kura didn't know where to look.

'Don't worry, bro. You borrow whatever you want of mine.' He held open the wardrobe door.

Kura picked a black rugby jersey. His cousins back home had warned him about the weather, but he hadn't believed them and wasn't prepared. He was about to put it on, when Abe said, 'Not that.' Abe took the rugby jersey from him and brushed the palm of his hand down both sides of it to iron out any new wrinkles he imagined were there, and draped it back on its hanger. Then he pulled a sweatshirt from one of the drawers. Kura pulled it over his head and shoulders, the fleece cowl cushioning the back of his neck. He hadn't realised how cold the back of his neck was until then.

It wasn't the sound of crowing roosters that woke Kura the next day. The bathroom door slamming, the gushing toilet bowl, six pairs of feet on the carpet in the corridor – none of these things would have roused him from sleep back home. He'd had a restless night, not helped by Abe's snoring or the cars he heard motoring past his window. The shock of waking up in an unfamiliar room did nothing to ease his nerves, and now he was expected to go to Mass. He followed Abe's lead and dragged himself out of bed. He pulled on the clothes that Tu had laid out for him, a mishmash of items from his brothers and father.

'You walk to church with the boys, OK, son?' Tu tucked Kura's collar down and straightened his tie. The formal clothing itched against his skin; he tugged at the shirt when she left the room.

'Looking flash, brother,' Abe teased. 'Like a Raro Elvis Presley, my bro.'

In the sitting room, Kura checked his reflection in the

framed Jesus print, turning his head to the right, then left, then right again, smoothing down the sides of his hair with his palms, his hands now greasy with the Brylcreem his father insisted he use. The slacks and shirt from Abe were two sizes too big, his legs like twigs within the fabric. His feet were close to bursting out of Moses' shoes, and the woollen vest from Joseph would give him a rash. His father's tie was suffocating.

The boys pounded the footpath ahead of him. Kura's feet were beginning to throb. He ignored the pain and eavesdropped on his brothers' conversation about rugby, knowing that even if he had something to say, he still would have contributed nothing. By the time they arrived at the church, the relief of resting his feet overshadowed his dread at facing the throng of strangers outside the building. For a moment.

'Aere mai, son,' said Tu. Again, Kura recoiled at the word 'son', his self-consciousness heightened in front of this crowd. His brothers were quick to disperse, hovering in the vicinity but never close enough for their mother to call on them. Tu held him gently by the elbow and led him to the door of the church, pulling him into the swarm of unknown faces. Of course he didn't recognise any of the parishioners – his mother's family weren't Catholic, and any cousins he'd grown up with who were about his age and lived in New Zealand were probably nursing hangovers.

'This is your Aunty Ina, my sister. And these are your cousins. Come, meet them.' Tu gestured to a woman in white, the garland of pink plastic hibiscuses in her hat distinguishing her from the other aunties. Aunty Ina grabbed him by the shoulders, stamped his cheek with a kiss and began introducing him to each of her children. They were reluctant to meet his eye, greeting him instead with the crowns of their heads. It pleased him to not have to baby talk with them.

He followed Tu through the heavy wooden doors and joined a smaller group crammed in the narthex. Doors to his left and right led to more seating upstairs. Later, he'd hear the choir in that upper level, delivering harmonies that could lift the roof clean, exposing the faithful to the heavens. The doors that opened onto the nave were set with stained glass windows, the holy family frozen inside mosaic panels. Suspended white halos, humbling robes, piety personified. Kura wasn't so much in awe of it all as intimidated by its sincerity. He stared at the rows of pews in front of him, so different from the ones back home. The pews here were made from oak, ensuring families a seat in this house for generations. The carpet was plush and a deep red, like fresh blood, moving Kura along the floor in waves. It carried him down the aisle, inching him towards the altar of white marble, where the crucified son of God towered despondently.

'Sit with me.' Any other day, the idea of Kura in a church on a Sunday was unthinkable. But today wasn't any other day. Tu turned, urging her children to join them, and when he heard them behind him, it surprised him to feel comforted.

He noticed his father once they were seated. Taki owned the church aisle as if he were God himself. He wore his Sunday best beneath his white catechist robe, and strutted as he walked. Then he ducked in and out of the vestry, placing chalices and offertory bowls on the credence table. When Taki walked past them again, he didn't seem to notice them. They ignored him back, as if it were part of a ritual.

Kura still couldn't see how this man was his father. They shared few similarities that he had noticed, and he doubted that time could heal the disconnection. Nothing had happened in nineteen years, after all; his rapport with Tu felt more important. Meeting his father had been a mistake. For him and his mother.

The parishioners in the pews in front of Kura addressed one another with familiarity, their enthusiasm abundant. Every now and then, they'd turn discreetly in their seats to glance at him. But Tu stared straight ahead at the giant crucifix. Kura wondered whether she'd already started praying.

Then she whispered to him. 'Here, son. Take this. It's yours.'

He looked down at the hymn book she'd handed him. He'd never owned a book before.

*

'This is my cousin . . . Takiora.'

'Tar-key-oh-rah?'

'No. Tah-kee-orr-rah.' Taki's cousin Vinnie enunciated Taki's Christian name so his boss, who could only speak English, would understand.

'Tarr-keyy-ohh . . . bloody hell.' The boss swore. 'You islanders and your full-on names.'

Taki flinched at 'islander'.

'Do you want a job?' the boss asked him.

Taki didn't trust his English and, besides, this man made him too nervous. He didn't speak.

'Are you a good worker?'

Taki barely managed to push a word past his throat. 'Yes.'

'He's a hard worker, boss,' said Vinnie. 'We worked

together in Makatea. That was real hard work, alright. Every day we had to—'

'I know, I know,' the boss said. 'You worked the guano deposits on the island and sent money back home to your parents. I've heard the story, Vinnie. You've told me a million times already.' The boss turned to Taki. 'I could use another good worker. I'll give you one week. Your cousin can show you the ropes. If I'm not happy with you, you're out. Fair?'

Taki nodded, smiling.

'Oh, and about your name . . . how's Tar-key sound?'

Taki was confused until Vinnie nudged him.

'Good,' he said. 'It's good.'

Taki had been in the country for only three days and already he had a job at the freezing works and a room in a boarding house on Majoribanks Street. Vinnie met him at the train station in Wellington, where the wind was crisp and strong and seemed to carry the crowds against their will. The tall concrete buildings of the city were officious and impersonal, and the roads seemed overrun with cars and trams and buses, the trams snaking their way from the train station towards Lambton Quay and finally down Courtenay Place, where life hurtled by. He had seen no other faces like his on that tram ride to the boarding house and, despite his cousin's company, he felt alone.

But the feeling, like life in the city, was fleeting.

'This is my cousin Takiora. Taki.' The men returned to the freezing works at Ngauranga, and Vinnie introduced him to the rest of the boys. Many of them were new here too. They welcomed him like a brother.

*

On Monday morning, the grey Cortina parked up outside the house. They told him they'd pick him up at 8am sharp, but Kura had never known his cousins to be punctual. He waited for them at the front door, expecting delays and untold excuses, so when they arrived promptly, blowing the horn and hollering his name, he felt disconcerted and needed a moment to find his bearings. There was little time to check he had everything: empty wallet, resume, comb. He looked at his feet and checked for smudges on his father's shoes, which he'd borrowed when Tu saw his blisters after church. His father's feet were oversized, and to aggravate matters the polish was wet still and it smelled.

'Make sure you get the polish into all the folds,' Taki had said. 'See how the leather is cracked? Get the polish right in but keep the polish even.' It felt like the first piece of fatherly advice Kura had received.

He could hear his siblings getting ready for school, lining up for the toilet, fighting over watered-down milk. A scuffle had broken out in the corridor, limbs flying as they karate-chopped the air. It wasn't until they wrestled each other to the carpet in hysterics that Kura realised they were only playing. Their father had left for the freezing works hours ago.

'Good luck, son.' Tu appeared beside him in the doorway and pulled him in for a hug. Kura struggled to relax into her affections, and when he heard his cousins' wolf whistles and caught Abe mocking him behind her back, he withdrew and watched as she threw a quick wave at the grey Cortina. The gesture shocked his cousins into silence, their windows rolling up.

Kura walked down the driveway and slid into the back seat of the car. 'We go to the pub now, cuz?' his cousin Lucy asked. The car filled with laughter, deep from the belly.

'Is that all you care about?' Kura said. 'Drinking your life away? Don't you know it's a sin to drink?' His cousins hung their heads, the car growing silent, until he couldn't keep a straight face any longer. They started laughing again, raising their voices and wisecracking.

As the car crawled down the street, Kura caught a glimpse of Tu waving out to them. Only when they turned the corner did she go back inside.

'How was church yesterday, cuz?' Tana called out from the driver's seat. 'Did you get saved by the Holy Spirit? Did your father forgive you your sins, my cuz? What happened to you after you showed up on Saturday?'

Kura told them about his siblings, especially Abe. He showed his cousins the resume Abe had helped him write, and the mocking resumed.

'You don't need that piece of paper, cuz,' said Tana. 'Just flash that beautiful smile at the rich old ladies. They'll look after you. A beautiful, exotic creature like yourself.'

Kura looked out the window in time to see the church disappear down the road. His cousins wolf-whistled at the building and dotted their chests and foreheads.

They drove for several minutes more before the concrete building towering over the hill came into view. Twice in two days Kura had been blown away by architecture.

'Is this it?'

'This is it, cuz,' said Tana. 'Say kia orana to your new home.'

'This is my cousin Kura,' Tana told his boss. The boss grabbed Kura's hand, his hold firm and assured. Kura, panicking, tried to hand over his resume. He'd neglected to unfold it first and it looked small and crumpled.

'What's this?' The boss sounded bemused as he unfolded the paper. 'Resume?' A grin spread slowly across his face. 'Fancy pants, eh? You wanna run this place or something?'

Tana jumped in. 'His father made him write that. He said for him to make a good impression.' His laugh was forced and not catching. 'But I can tell you, boss, my cousin – he's a hard worker.'

The boss looked at Kura. 'You do everything your daddy tells you, kid?'

Kura wanted to tell this man that he barely knew his father, that he'd only met him two days ago and he didn't think he liked him. He wasn't certain he could obey Taki; his gut told him he wouldn't. His head told him his father didn't want him there, that it had been Tu who had coaxed him into writing that letter. But his heart wasn't sure. His mother had seen something in his father at one time. He had to hold on to that.

'Can you talk?'

'He's just a bit shy, boss,' Tana said.

'You gotta be able to talk to the other workers, boy.'

'He will,' said Tana. 'He can. I'll show him. I'll help him talk to the others, boss. You'll see.'

The boss paused for a long time. 'Things are tight round here. I can't take every Tom, Dick and Harry. I need someone who can hit the ground running.' He looked at Kura again. 'Can you run, boy?'

Kura couldn't see the point in running, especially if he was going to be building cars.

'He's fast, boss,' said Tana. 'You watch. I'll show him.'

Kura didn't know what to say and even if he did, he didn't think he had the voice to say it.

'Look at him,' the boss said with a sneer. 'The boy can

barely look at me.'

Kura's head weighed on him like rocks; he struggled to lift it.

'Count yourself lucky you don't have to work for him,' Tana was saying.

Kura stared beyond the horizon, into the city at the foot of the hill. The buildings and cars below looked like a backdrop to a movie scene. But this wasn't just a dream now.

'That man's a bastard, cuz. You're better off.'

Kura stopped listening. His mind had skipped ahead to the interrogation at his father's house. Where is your job? When do you start? When can you start paying your way? He hadn't noticed that Tana had stopped talking, until he spoke again.

'You need some money for the bus, cuz? I can give you some money to get home if you want?'

Kura already knew where the spare key was hidden.

'Four pot plants to the left of the back door. Just until we can get your own key cut.' Tu had thought of everything.

But Kura couldn't return to his father's house, not yet. For starters, only Tu would be there, with the baby, and he couldn't impose any more than he already had. Not that she would've minded.

'I'll walk,' he said.

'It's a long way, cuz.'

'I have all day.'

Tana sounded remorseful. 'I thought I could help.'

Kura tried to ease the tension. 'Maybe I go to the pub now, eh?'

'Have one for me, cuz.'

*

After a year, Taki had settled into a routine. The men at the freezing works worked hard for their money, so on Friday nights the young ones like Taki made their way into town. This Friday was no different.

'Taki!'

'Yeah?'

'How 'bout a beer, mate?'

Taki looked down at his lemonade. He didn't drink, and the boys gave him a hard time for it.

'No, thank you, my friend. I got my beer here.' He raised his soft drink at Joe, who'd started at the freezing works after Vinnie had left five months ago. Despite their different backgrounds – Joe was born and bred just south of Rotorua – he and Taki had become good friends.

'C'mon, mate.' Joe's ribbing was constant. 'You're not in church now. God will still let you in Heaven if you have one beer.'

An uproar from the men filled their corner. Taki turned to them. 'Look at him,' he said, gesturing at Joe. 'He thinks he's Eve, leading poor Adam into temptation with a beer. But I didn't know Eve was this ugly.' He didn't mind being the centre of attention, so he liked it when the other men laughed at his jokes. It helped keep his mind off his business back home. His son had turned two, and it was two years since his wife had died.

'Ugly?' Joe said. 'Mate, your dark good looks might turn the ladies' heads, but unless you know how to lead them into temptation – forget it, my friend.'

Actually, it was Taki who led Joe into temptation.

The following Wednesday, Taki invited Joe to a church social in Newtown. It was a weekly event and thrumming with local islanders. When they reached the church hall, the deep bass of the island melodies was already flooding the streets.

Taki glanced over at his fair-skinned friend. His blond curls were slicked back with too much hair oil. His face, though smooth, had a speck of blood on it. His shoes, freshly polished, concealed the creases in the leather, though only just. But it was his suit that made Taki's heart sink. The seat of his pants that rode too high up, the muted shade of grey that drained his complexion. Why did his friend make no effort?

'Be careful, mate,' Taki said to him. 'These island girls aren't like your Kiwi girls.' He watched Joe's tense smile. 'They might like you.' He elbowed Joe in the ribs as they entered the hall, searching the room for a familiar face. When he recognised no one, they huddled in a corner. Toe-tapping. Self-conscious. And then came the women. Taki introduced Joe.

'Kia orana, Joe.' A sultry island woman greeted the nervous newcomer. 'My name is Helena and this is my friend, Kai.' Beside her, Kai lowered her eyes. Joe did the same. Taki resisted the urge to mock him.

Taki and the women danced while Joe bounced from foot to foot. The women swayed their hips and moved their hands suggestively as Taki closed in on Helena, his limbs synchronised with the beats. He danced with the tempo, his movements blending with the music, while Joe continued to bounce out of time. He bounced from one island song into the next, and before they both knew it, it was time to go home.

'I think Kai likes you, mate,' Taki teased. They were walking down Adelaide Road, the cool air like glass.

'Course she does.' Joe combed a hand through his hair.

'I didn't know you could dance like that,' said Taki. 'No wonder she likes you.'

They walked the rest of the way in silence.

*

It was nearly nine when Kura reached the bottom of the hill. He crossed the road to the main shopping area, wishing he'd eaten more than two slices of toast. Tu had offered to cook him some eggs, but he couldn't eat in front of the others. He remembered them fighting over the milk, and how they watered it down to make it last. The taste of it didn't bother him – he was used to powdered milk back home – but it mattered to his siblings, whose taste buds had been trained to want more. He ignored his rumbling stomach as he dawdled along the rows of shops, stopping every now and then to peek through the windows.

'Kura? That you, nephew?' Kura didn't recognise the woman's voice, but she spoke in Cook Islands Māori and the words put him at ease. He turned as Aunty Ina rushed towards him, her grip tight on his arms when she finally reached him. 'What are you doing here?' Her kiss on his cheek was resolute.

He spoke in his own language. 'Work, Aunty. I'm looking for work.'

'Ah, yes,' she said. Kura felt exposed. Had she and Tu discussed this already? He thought again about the watered-down milk. The need to find work weighed heavily on him. He hadn't expected a land of watered-down milk and honey. His father had neglected to warn him in his letter.

It's time, the letter had said. *Come to New Zealand. Here,*

you will find work, make good money. Send money back home,
help your mother's family. Build a life here, you have brothers
and sisters ready to meet you. His mother's sister back home
had agreed. 'Some of your cousins can make over a hundred
dollars in a week,' she'd said. 'Stay with your father. He's an
important man over there. He will help you settle in.'

Kura looked down at his father's shoes; the polish was
losing its shine.

'Any luck?'

'Still looking, Aunty.'

'Chin up, boy. Something will show.'

'Yoo-hoo!' Kura turned to watch a woman bounding
down the street towards them. She reminded him of a
bulldog. He recognised her vaguely from yesterday's Mass –
another woman in the family he had to get used to.

'Hello, Elizabeth.' Aunty Ina drew out her name,
emphasising each syllable.

'Kia orana, Kura,' Elizabeth said, ignoring her. Kura's
shoulders tensed up when she kissed him. 'How are you, my
boy? How's your mum?' she asked. 'Your stepmum, I mean.
Your father's wife. How is she today?'

Aunty Ina stared blankly.

Kura used his English words. 'She's good, Aunty.'

She turned to Aunty Ina. 'It must be hard for your sister
having another mouth to feed.' She paused dramatically.
'Oh no,' she corrected herself, 'she wanted another baby,
didn't she?' She turned back to Kura. 'You're a lifesaver, boy.
She's been wanting another kid to look after, even though
she already has a baby. Baby machine, that one.'

Aunty Ina said, 'We see you around, Elizabeth,' and
pulled Kura down the street. 'She's a troublemaker, boy,' she
whispered. 'Stay away from her.'

Kura's stomach rumbled again, and he looked away when he saw she'd noticed. 'Hasn't my sister been feeding you?'

'Yes, Aunty, of course.' He was quick to respond. 'She's very good to me.'

They stopped outside the post office building. 'This is where I work,' she said. The building stood out amongst the other businesses, raised from the ground level, forcing customers to climb its steps. Kura was impressed. He didn't know anyone who worked in an office; he thought she must be the first in the family. 'Come and visit me whenever you like. I work on the front counter, just wave out to me.'

They both knew he wouldn't.

'Don't be shy. We're family now.' Before she left, Aunty Ina pressed a ten-dollar note into the palm of his hand. 'Go buy yourself some food. You're going to need your strength today.'

Kura found a bench and rested his feet. His father's shoes were an improvement on his brother's, but the soles were too rigid. He wrapped his fingers round the ten-dollar note, feeling like a billionaire. There were iced cakes in the window of the bakery in front of him. He caught a whiff of the mince pies and looked at the note in his hand. He hoped it was enough.

'Can I help you?'

Kura knew what he wanted to say but whether he could say it was another story. Through the glass of the pie warmer he eyed up a pie in the front row. The smell of the pastry was mouth-watering, but the only noise he could muster was the rumble from his gut.

'This will fix that,' said the baker. He reached into the back of the warmer and pulled out a pie with a pair of tongs. 'They're very good,' he gloated. 'Best in town.' He waited for Kura to respond, and when he finally did, he slipped the pie into a brown paper bag and handed it over to Kura, who swapped it for the ten-dollar note. The pie was warm in his hand. He was careful to be gentle with it.

Sitting on the bench outside, he bit through the pastry. The meat was tender and drowning in gravy, and the pastry was like nothing he'd tasted back home. He stuffed it too fervently into his mouth and it wasn't long before he was down to the last bite. His stomach had stopped rumbling, but he could easily have wolfed down a second pie.

His energy had returned, enough to make the long trek back to his father's house. It wouldn't be difficult to find – two main streets, a church and some shops. If he took his time, he could arrive at the house just before five.

*

Before long, Taki was the strongest worker at the boning table.

'Taki! How 'bout another challenge, mate?'

He looked over at Joe. 'Aren't you sick of losing yet?'

The men on the floor laughed.

'You scared I'm gonna win this time?' said Joe. 'You know I let you win cos I feel sorry for you.'

Taki shrugged. 'Nah, too busy.' He leaned against the edge of the boning table, folding his arms and crossing his legs. 'See? Busy. Maybe I beat you some other time.' He beamed as the men watching laughed again.

'How 'bout a little wager then?'

Taki couldn't resist a gamble. He knew Joe was well aware of this. But he said, 'I can't do that, my friend. Too easy. Like stealing your money. And I couldn't call myself a good

Christian then.' The banter was rife today.

'Not money – *lunch*.'

Taki considered the stakes. Working here guaranteed all the sausages you could eat. The work was hard and made an island fulla hungry. You had to keep your strength up and your mind on the job. But there were only so many sausages he could eat.

'Okay,' said Taki. 'But only so you can save face in front of the boys. Or try to. That's only fair.'

'*Taaa*-ki!'

'*Taaa*-ki!'

The men were gathered round the boning table, watching Taki and Joe strip a carcass each, and cheering on Taki – the reigning champ. Beads of sweat formed on his brow as he hacked away at the lamb's corpse. He was leading; a heap of meat cuts were piled to one side and his knife slid effortlessly through the flesh of the dead animal. It had taken him nine years to master this skill. He glanced at Joe, who looked frantic and beaten, his knife cuts jagged.

Later, Taki licked the salt from his fingers and took a swig from his bottle of lemonade. He raised his drink to Joe across the table. 'Cheers, mate.' He looked down at the battered fish and the few chips left in front of him, then at the sausages on Joe's plate. Be careful what you wish for, he thought, remembering his first meal in New Zealand.

*

By the time Kura reached the TAB at the Cannons Creek shops, it was well after midday. He'd never been a gambling man, never saw the point of it. It felt senseless and wasteful, and also he lacked the funds. But he still had several hours before he could show his face at his father's house, and since the TAB looked close to deserted he entered the dark, smoke-filled room and burrowed into one of the corners. The punters, several men and one woman, had their eyes glued to the race lists on the walls. Kura watched them make their way to the counter to bet, then as they listened intently to the commentary from the speakers. They were motionless as the booming voice filled the space. Kura studied them. Their concentration was exemplary, all eyes and ears on the speakers above them. It was a different kind of praying, but just as earnest as the kind he'd witnessed yesterday; they believed in what each race could deliver for them.

But the hope in their eyes was fading. Nearly all of their horses crossed the line in fourth place or worse. Kura imagined too keenly their loss, which was more than monetary. Only one man cheered, sauntering back to the counter to collect his winnings. And Kura knew that later, the others would slink back to their cars, or walk home, broke and broken.

Just after four, his father arrived. Kura quickly turned his back to him. There were just enough other men in the room to keep him hidden. He glanced over as Taki swotted the race lists, comparing each one with the names in his *Best Bets.* Eyes still on his magazine, he made his way to the counter, placed his bet, then turned towards the speakers. He was so engrossed in the commentary that even if Kura had been standing right next to him he doubted his father would notice. Taki's expression became more animated and he raised his arms in victory as the horses turned the final corner. His smile was wide. But then his face dropped. His mouth snapped shut and his arms fell forlornly to his sides. Kura watched his father tear up his tickets.

Kura slipped out of the TAB. On his way home, he went to the dairy and bought two bottles of milk.

'When do you start?' asked Taki.

Kura looked up from his plate.

'Your job. When do you start your job?'

Tu put one of the bottles of milk on the table and smiled over at Kura in gratitude. 'Leave the boy alone,' she said. 'He just got here. He has time. Look at what he bought us.' She held up the bottle. Kura felt ashamed, more so when he saw the guilt on his father's face. 'Anyway,' she said, 'why can't he just sign up for the dole?'

Taki was adamant. 'No son of mine will live on handouts.'

The next day, the grey Cortina arrived promptly. Kura made sure he had his new resume with him. Abe had helped him tweak it the night before.

'Helped your grandad on the taro plantation? Gardener. Your nana made you climb the fruit trees for cooking? Chef. You cycled by pushbike all over the island? Can use heavy machinery. Don't worry, bro,' Abe had said. 'You'll find something.' Kura felt bolstered by his brother's words.

The cousins dropped him off at the town centre before driving up the hill to Todd's. 'Just go in and ask, cuz,' said Tana. 'Use that island charm of yours.'

Kura could still hear their teasing as they drove off.

He sat on the bench outside the bakery. He didn't want to bump into Aunty Ina again. There were few people in the area, mainly workers, and as soon as the doors to the bakery opened, he went in.

'Good morning, my friend,' said the baker. Kura tried to smile. 'Another pie? Or maybe a cream doughnut?' He pointed at the shelf of cream doughnuts dusted in icing sugar.

Kura was tempted, but he hesitated. Then he reached into his pocket and pulled out his resume. He unfolded it and smoothed out the creases, then handed it to the baker, studied his face.

'Are you looking for a job?'

Kura nodded. 'Yes,' he said. 'I'm a hard worker.'

The baker paused. 'I'm sure you are, my friend.' His words put Kura at ease. But then he said, 'I can't afford to take on anyone else.' The look of pity on the baker's face hurt more than the rejection.

Kura took back his resume and stuffed it into his pocket. 'Okay,' he said, and he swept out the door, knowing he wouldn't come back here again.

The fresh air on his face gave him some relief. He just needed to keep moving.

'Still nothing?'

The family ate in silence.

Later, in their bedroom, Abe tried to build him back up. 'Look, bro, you just gotta be confident. Look these suckers in the eye and say, "You need me to work for you. Don't take too long, cos—"'

'I shouldn't have come here.' Kura's voice was a whisper. 'It's too hard for people like me.'

'What's that supposed to mean?' Abe snapped. 'No brother of mine gives up. It's not in our blood to quit.' Then he lowered his voice. 'You want me to come with you, bro?'

Kura could see that his offer was sincere, but he hated knowing his brother felt like his keeper.

'No,' he said. 'I'll be fine.'

*

Every year, the freezing works threw a picnic for its workers. Queen Elizabeth Park in Paekākāriki, twenty minutes north of Porirua, hummed all day with workers' families. Taki admired Abe at the starting blocks; his older son, Kura, was just a couple years older. He wondered whether Kura was athletic like Abe, and whether they shared similar outlooks. 'See my boy?' he said to Joe. 'It's not just his good looks he gets from his dad.'

Joe's arms were folded confidently across his chest. 'Don't be so sure, mate. My girl's in the running, too.' Taki turned to check out Joe's daughter. She was tall and slim, like a greyhound. And from what he'd heard about her from Joe, smart and tenacious. But so was Abe.

The clapper sounded and the race was on. There were twelve children running in this age group, and Abe was second to Joe's daughter. Joe winked at Taki.

'C'mon, boy,' Taki yelled. 'Get in there!'

Taki had never lost a challenge to Joe; he wasn't about to start losing now.

'C'mon, boy! You can do it!'

Halfway through the race, Joe's daughter was still leading and still gaining ground. But the resolve on Abe's face gave Taki hope. His son pounded the ground with long, unwavering steps. Joe's girl was still ahead, but only by a stride, and as they approached the finish line Taki called out again. His voice was the loudest at that park. Abe's arms and fists punched the air as he bounded towards the finish line. It was as if Taki's words were adding more drive to his pace, pushing him onwards to win.

The winner's ribbon was pinned proudly on the wall in the sitting room. It became a treasured family possession for years – third only to the velvet painting of Jesus, and second to the family portrait.

*

Kura's cousins dropped him off at the town centre the next day. Abe had talked him up so much that when he arrived in town, he was bent on visiting every shop.

By lunchtime, they'd all rejected him. 'It's not in our blood to quit,' Abe had told him, but he wondered if that mattered, that they shared the same blood. He wasn't convinced that quitting was bad, not when the expectations were already low.

By four thirty, his father's shoes were scuffed, their shine gone. He was exhausted and hungry, and the rejections had turned his stomach to rock. He no longer cared what the baker thought of him. He returned to the bakery and bought a pie, and sat outside on the bench to eat it.

It was as fine as the first one, filling and satisfying, warming his stomach.

By the end of the week, Kura was ready to quit. When his cousins dropped him off as usual, he walked back to the Cannons Creek shops, which took him twenty minutes. No point in dawdling or trying to kill time. He made his way to the Top Tavern and waited for it to open. He had a five dollar note left, plus change.

Taki was waiting for him when he got home that evening.

'Are you drunk? Again?'

Kura didn't answer.

'Is this what you do all day? Is this how you look for work?'

The room was circling, pulling Kura inwards like a draining sinkhole.

'Where did you get the money to drink?' Taki twisted Kura's collar tight around his fingers. Kura could feel his energy depleting.

'What are you doing? This is your son!'

At Tu's words, Taki let Kura go, watched him gasp for air. He turned to his wife, then skulked off to their bedroom. The door slammed behind him.

By Saturday, Kura had been living at his father's house for a week. He managed to avoid Taki in the morning, as the family had already left for Taki's work picnic. As usual, Kura's cousins picked him up, and he introduced them to Abe, who was riding with them because the family car was full. By the time they arrived at Queen Elizabeth Park, the races were starting.

'It's a good thing these races are grouped by age,' JJ, one of the younger workers, was telling Taki, 'or you'd never win yourself an ice block, mate. Lucky your wife's packed a decent feed for you jokers, or you'd starve.'

Kura's father had never backed down from a challenge. Ten minutes later he was lined up at the starting block, barefoot and stripped down to his singlet. Tu was looking wildly at him but he ignored her. At least he had the sense to save his shirt from ruin.

'C'mon, old man,' JJ goaded him at the starting line. 'Show me how it's done.'

'Ready, set!'

Taki and JJ led the race neck and neck. Taki seemed to relish the attention he was getting, the cheers of the older men at the picnic.

Kura watched Taki outrun his younger colleague, the crowd rallying behind him as he basked in the limelight. To everyone's surprise, though, another runner was vying for the win. Taki watched Abe run ahead of him, crossing the line to finish first.

Kura was waiting at the car for Abe. When his brother arrived, he was followed by Taki, who towered over him.

'Have you been drinking?' Taki sniffed the air.

Abe struggled to make words. Instead, he laughed.

'Why are you laughing?' His colleagues were watching them, and Abe's laughing was grating. Taki sniffed the air around him again, and lowered his voice. 'Are you drunk? Like your brother?'

Then he spotted Kura. He stormed towards him. 'What have you done with my son?'

Kura was silent; the beer and weed had slowed his reflexes. But the longer Kura refused to speak, the more it irritated his father. 'What's wrong with you? Speak!'

Tu raced over to where the men were standing. 'Taki!' she cried, but Taki ignored her. He was shouting now. 'What have you done with my son?'

Despite the attention they were getting, Taki couldn't stop himself. Before Kura could react, his whole body shook with the impact of his father's knuckles cracking the bone in his cheek.

*

Plenty had happened for Taki in nine years. He'd come a long way since arriving in New Zealand. He was still working at the freezing works and up for a promotion, and, like in those early days, his nerves were rife.

'Well done, Tar-key. We're impressed with your work here. You're a loyal, hard worker, and popular with the lads. And as you know,' the boss continued, 'we're offering the role to you or Joe. The work is more time-consuming and you'll take on more responsibility. Of course, as foreman, you'll be supervising the boys.'

The boss was watching him. Taki didn't flinch. Good.

'And then there's the paperwork – orders to fill and all that. I don't think you'll have a problem, and, just between us, I'd rather give it to you. But tell me what you think.'

Taki breathed deeply, trying to swallow the lump that snagged in his throat. Even after nine years, this man still made him nervous.

'Thank you, boss. But I can't accept it. I'm happy where I am. This is more than I dreamed of. A beautiful wife and family, a good job, my own home – what do I need a promotion for?'

The boss gaped. 'But the extra money? You have a growing family—'

'More money would be nice, but what price do I pay? Time away from my wife and family, time away from my home. Thank you, boss, but I'm happy where I am.'

He could tell the boss didn't understand Taki's logic. But he shook his head – if that's what he wanted. 'Okay, Tar-key. I'll tell Joe.'

*

Tu was watching Taki change the dressing on his hand.

'You remember when you turned down that job?' she said.

Taki remembered. He'd come home and told her, cradled the family Bible to comfort himself. Ran his eyes over the words, which looked like foreign shapes, every now and then finding a word he recognised. But the words he knew were too few and far between to make sense. It frustrated him as much as turning down that job had.

'You remember what you said when you told me you lost that job?' Tu said.

Taki said nothing. He couldn't look at her.

'You said, "We're doing all right the way we are." Do you think I didn't know you lied to me then? Do you think I didn't know the shame you felt?'

When Abe was old enough, he'd taught Taki to read and write. And when he'd written that letter to Kura, it was Tu who'd convinced him to do it. He still didn't know what kind of father he would be to him, or if he could close the gap he'd created.

Kura stood on the doorstep on Monday morning, waiting for his cousins. His eye was still bruised, and he needed to escape. His siblings were at school and Tu was bustling around inside, the baby still asleep.

Then his father came out and stood beside him. Kura braced himself.

'For you,' said Taki, and held something out to him.

Kura looked down. A key to the house.

Love Rules for Island Boys

If she's an island girl, find out who her brothers are. Do this first before you waste too much time. Don't worry about her old man – he doesn't know you exist. Worry about the women in her life: her mama, her aunties, her sisters and cousins.

When she comes to your house, make room for the cousin. She is the gatekeeper and you'll need her approval. So laugh at her jokes but don't try to outwit her. And when she gives you the side-eye, don't give it back. Don't be a smartarse. Don't make sudden movements. Just sit on your couch and watch Netflix.

Later, go to the kitchen and make you a feed. Cook like you're feeding a village in a hurricane. Stay away from the carrot sticks. Don't bother with the rice crackers. And, for the love of God, don't serve them no fruit. This apple slice is plenty, said no island girl ever. If you're going to feed her, feed her like your mama's watching.

If there's leftover takeaways, heat that up in the microwave. Chinese is good but KFC is your best option.

Feed her the chicken always in this order: thigh, drumstick, wings, breast, back.

Wait. Don't feed her the back. You may as well feed her bones. Skinny bones at that, with hardly any chicken skin, let alone meat. If that's all you've got, make her some toast. Maybe cook her some eggs. Fried eggs. Scrambled eggs. Poached eggs. Boiled eggs. However she wants it, make it that way. Cook those chicken eggs like it's your life's mission. And never ever tell her to cook *you* some eggs, *woman*.

If you still live at home, don't tell her that, either. If you still live at home, you will need to do some prep work. Don't skip any of the following steps.

Take down from the walls all the velvet paintings of Jesus. If you had any, remove any school certificates also. She doesn't need to know you can swim a full lap or hold your breath underwater or float on your back. Family photos, nativity scenes, plastic flowers, woven mats and baskets, rosary beads, shell necklaces, the family Bible, crucifixes, the tīvaevae covers on the cushions, the plastic sheet on the couch – all of these things must go.

If she's a smart girl, throw some books on the coffee table. If she likes sport, flex your muscles where she can see them. If she's a music lover, serenade her with an island song. Play your father's ukulele and tell her you carved it from scratch. Show her the machete from the toolbox in the toolshed and make sure you return it before your dad gets home.

If you've played your cards right, the cousin will approve. She will turn her side-eye into a blind eye when you decide you want some privacy. Hand the cousin the TV remote and make your way to another room. Take the girl with you. She'll follow your lead now.

Turn the radio on. Shut the curtains. Pull the bed back from the wall.

Her cousin won't mind waiting.

*

If she's a white girl, find out who her father is. Do this first in case you have to meet him. When she comes to your house, she'll be by herself, but her girlfriend will drop her off down the street. Beware of the girlfriend and know she's not far. She's the white girl equivalent to island girl cousin.

When she's standing on your doorstep, tell her she can leave her shoes on. She'll insist that she wants to be treated the same. This will make you laugh, but don't laugh on the outside. Do laugh at her jokes, though, and pretend to outwit her. It's a little like foreplay, and she'll thank you for it later.

Don't heat up the leftovers – she's allergic to fat. She thinks killing animals for food is cruel, and she's also on a raw food diet. When she's around, you're vegetarian too. So bring on those carrot sticks. Pull the hummus out from the back of the fridge. Eat fruit to your heart's content. But only if she's feeling peckish.

Because – let's be honest – she didn't come here to eat.

Turn the radio on. Shut the curtains. Pull the bed back from the wall.

Afterwards, sit on your couch and watch Netflix. Leave the house as it is. She likes that you still live at home with your folks. She adores your mama's tīvaevae cushion covers. She loves that you have a spiritual side. She thinks the plastic sheet on the couch is *culturally enlightening*. She's never seen anything like it in the books she's read at university – and she is very widely read, she will let you know.

She'll tell you her parents want to meet you. Don't panic – you'll startle her and she'll wonder why she embarrasses you. Tell her she doesn't and of course you want to meet them.

Because they'll want to see the house you grew up in. They've never actually been inside a state housing unit before.

They expect it'll be a hoot, and they can't wait to tell all their friends back at the country club. You don't actually know if they belong to a country club, but one racist stereotype deserves another.

You don't live in a state house. You've never lived in a state house. You think about borrowing your mate's one for the day – the one he paid a million dollars for and is renting out at seven hundred dollars a week. But you don't need to impress them in this way. It will thrill them enough just to be in a place like the Creek. They pride themselves on their open-mindedness. One of their best friends is Somalian – and by that they mean people like you.

If she's a white girl, your mama will have a say in it. Be prepared.

Bluey

My cousin told me that house is a tinny house. That's a stupid name for a house made of wood, I said. And she said I was stupid so now we ain't cousins no more. I reckon she meant roof – tinny roof – cos that's the only tin on that wooden house I can see.

'Lock the doors, bub. Keep them locked, remember. Don't open the doors for no one, K? Stranger danger, don't forget.'

Dad wouldn't leave me alone until I locked the doors so I leaned over and pushed down the button on his side of the car. The locks went click and then I watched Dad walk up the drive towards the tinny roof. He turned back to check on me before he disappeared round the back.

The car key was still in the hole. I turned it twice towards Dad's window like I'd seen him do and the radio made some scratchy noise. Then I pressed the buttons on the radio until the golden oldies station came up. Dad listens to the songs from the olden days cos it makes him remember when things were easy. I listen to them cos I have no choice, and now I think they're not that bad. But I'll never tell my dad that. I knew the song on the radio from Nanny and Papa's place. They sing it all bloody night when they're on the piss under the blue plastic at the back of the house. Dad says I'm too young to swear, but what he don't know won't hurt him, I reckon. So I turned up the radio and sang my bloody heart out.

'*Wasted days and wasted nights . . .*' When I didn't know the words I just hummed along. There were other cars in the street and people coming and going, coming and going. But all that mattered to me right then was getting wasted all day and night . . . but not for real. Cos getting wasted means drinking too much piss and singing old songs too loud with a guitar, and my papa says I have to be at least fourteen.

Nanny and Papa buy their piss from Uncle Anaru, who sells it for five dollars per Coke bottle and calls it his Raro homebrew. That's cheap, he tells Papa. Family rates. The real thing too, he says – just like the good stuff back home. Nanny and Papa must reckon he's right cos they buy four bottles of Raro homebrew from Uncle Anaru and four bags of Raro doughnuts for the same price from Aunty Polly every Friday night. Then Nanny goes to housie and Papa has to wait for her to come home before he's allowed to get wasted. If I'm sleeping over, like tonight, then I'll go to housie too. You're my lucky charm, says Nanny. And if the Holy Spirit has been kind to her, she might bring home a meat pack or the twenty dollars she's won back on her housie cards. If it's a meat pack, then there'll be rump steak and doughnuts for breakfast the next day.

Papa's favourite song came on next. He loves country western. I can tell the singer is a white man cos how many cowboys with rhinestones you know are brown? I asked Nanny what rhinestones were and she showed me her wedding ring and hard out it's the most beautiful thing. More beautiful than the glass rosary beads Nanny and Papa gave me for my birthday. This will protect you, my nanny said. She didn't say from what. I wore it to school once, like it was a string of rhinestones, and Mum beat me with the island broom. Not too hard cos I was just a dumb six-year-old, but hard enough that I wouldn't do it again. None of the men in my family wear sparkles like that. None of the men in my family own cowboy hats.

I was still singing about white cowboys when Dad came back to the car.

'Open the door, bub.'

He knocked on the window three times. There was him and this fulla that I didn't know. He was black as.

'Rosie,' said Dad, 'open the door.' He knocked three times again and it made me think of a song. *Knock three times on the ceil—*

'Rosie!'

They weren't going nowhere so I leaned over and pulled the buttons back up. I left Dad's door to last so I had to unlock each door one by one. The wind blew through the car when Dad opened his door and he took up the whole doorway.

'Rosie, this is my mate Bluey. Say hello.'

I looked over at my dad's mate Bluey. He wasn't family. He was too fat to play rugby with Dad. I would know if he was from around here. I didn't know this man from a bar of soap. That's what my Nanny says. So why the bloody hell should I say hello? Stranger danger. I looked straight ahead at the road. There was only one other car in the street now. Even the rhinestone cowboy was gone from the radio.

'Rosie.' Dad's voice went hard. 'Say hello to Bluey, and get in the back seat.'

I turned my eyeballs to Bluey. Like I said, he was fat. His dreadlocks looked like dirty ropes. His clothes were black. His skin was black. His eyes were brown. His teeth were yellow – what teeth he had left. The gap where his two front teeth should've been made him look like a baby. *Bluey*. What a stupid name.

'Nah, nah, bro,' Bluey said, 'it's all good, eh. I can sit in the back seat.'

'Rosie,' Dad said, 'get in the back seat. *Now*.'

By the time I went to move to the back seat, Bluey already had one leg inside the car. He had some old black trackpants on, the kind that go in at the ankles.

'All good, bro,' he said. 'More room in the back seat, eh?'

I knew Dad was giving me the eye. 'Bluey,' he said, not taking the eye off me, 'this is my daughter, Rosie. She takes after her mother.'

Bluey laughed. It made the back of my neck itch. He laughed like a girl – a fat, black, dirty, toothless baby girl. Dad was still staring at me so I turned to stare back at him but there was a chubby hand in the way. Bluey's fingernails were too long for a man, and the dirt underneath them looked like the black side of half-moons.

'Nice to meet you, Rosie.'

I let Bluey shake my fingers. His hands were sweaty.

'Faarr, bro! This is a flash car, my bro. Look at these things, bro. *Electric windows*, bro!'

The window behind me went *whirr* then stopped. *Whirr.* Stop. *Whirr.* Stop.

'Gets us from A to B. That's all we need. A to B.' Dad turned the radio down.

'One foot in front of the other, eh, bro.'

Some kids were playing rugby on the road. They stopped just long enough for us to pass.

'When Rosie's older, I'll teach her how to drive. Then she can pick me up at the pub.' I knew Dad wanted me to look at him so I could laugh with him, but he knows I hate it when people make fun of me. Served him right if his feelings got hurt.

'Must be my lucky day, my bro, running into you like that.'

'It's been ages since I seen you, bro. Not since . . .' Dad went quiet. 'School days.'

'What school do you go to, Rosie?'

Only my family called me Rosie, cos they know me better than anyone. If I had a best friend at school, even she wouldn't call me Rosie. She'd call me Rosita. I would make sure of it.

'Can your daughter talk, bro?' Bluey leaned over to Dad's side. 'Fuck that, bro,' he said, looking at me out the side of his face. 'She's too young to be a dumb mute.'

When I fight with my cousins we call each other stupid and dumb. It's the worst thing you can call someone. It means you think you're better than them and when you think that about someone you love they may as well be a ghost.

'Maraeroa,' said Dad. 'Primer three.'

'Far, man.' Bluey tried to whistle through the gap in his teeth. It sounded like wet wind. 'What a brainy box.' The car went quiet for about a minute and I could tell Dad didn't like it. Some people are too scared to talk in their heads. They'd rather talk about the weather than be quiet for a minute.

'Remember when we were at school?' said Dad. 'Things have changed a bit since then.'

'I only lasted that one year at college, bro. Hardly even counts.' Bluey let out more wet wind. 'I remember your mum, Rosie. She was pretty as, your mum.'

Usually I don't mind being quiet for a minute but I wished I had something to say about that.

'She was the prettiest girl at school. She looked a lot like you, eh, Rosie.'

I could feel my face getting warm. I opened my window. *Whirr.* Stop.

'Fuck she was smart.' Then he said sorry. 'Didn't mean to swear.'

Dad waved his hand as if swearing was OK now. 'Nothing Rosie hasn't already heard.'

I turned in my seat. 'Were you in Mum's class, too?'

Bluey's eyes went big as the moon. He stared at me then Dad then me. 'Yep,' he said. 'All three of us were in the same class. Just in the third form, though, cos I . . . left early.'

His moon eyes got glassy. I turned back to the front cos it's none of my business to watch a grown man cry. We passed some brick houses that looked like brick jails, and houses with no upstairs that looked like yawning boxes.

'Bluey and his family lived next door to your nanny and papa's. We were next-door neighbours for ages, eh, bro?'

'Yeah, bro. My old man always said youse were the best bungas he knew. Oh—' He paused. 'Sorry, bro. I didn't mean bungas – I meant *coconuts*.'

Dad laughed and I gave him the eye. 'My dad always said you horis were OK, too.' They both cracked up like they were back in the third form.

I turned in my seat again and looked into Bluey's moon eyes. 'Did you know Mum's family?'

'Yes,' he said. 'I beat up her older brother. Fucker tried to pash my girlfriend.'

'That's Uncle Davey! He has a boyfriend now.'

'*Fuck* – did I beat up a faggot?'

'No, you beat up my *uncle*.'

'Careful, bro. That's her favourite uncle.'

'Sorry, miss. Me and my big fat mouth.'

It felt like we'd been driving for ages before I noticed the turn-off for the motorway.

'Dad,' I said, staring down the open road, 'where we going?'

'Adventure, girl.'

The car picked up speed.

'Don't forget to drop me off. It's housie night.'

There weren't any brick jails or yawning boxes on the motorway. Just road and grass and signs and cars. I couldn't tell what time it was – it was hard to tell when the days got sunnier. All I knew was that housie started at six and Nanny left home at five thirty on the dot and I finished school at three and we would've spent at least ten minutes at the tinny roof.

'Don't forget, Dad. Nanny will be waiting for me.'

'Hey, bro, remember when we used to . . . Remember when we used to go into town for . . . *a movie*?' Bluey said.

'Yeah, bro. I remember those days.'

I couldn't remember the last time Dad took me to the movies. The last movie I saw was about a boy and his turtle. I cried at the end and so did my nanny. But Nanny cried cos she misses the islands. That's where the movie was made.

'You, me and Juju were thick as thieves back then.' Bluey poked his head round my seat. I smelt onion on his breath. 'That's what we called your mum back then, Rosie. Cos she had the biggest juju lips at school.'

I pressed my lips together and checked my face in the

side mirror. I looked like Kermit the Frog with my no-lips. Then Bluey's face was in the side mirror, too. We both looked away at the same time.

'I mean, we called her Juju cos her name was June. Juju for short.' I looked at him in the mirror again and he was looking back at me and didn't look away. His moon eyes turned into bung eyes.

We passed Tawa and then J-ville. I looked out for the road signs. Dad showed me how to read road signs since when I was little. And maps and other things like the names of towns. Follow the Ones and keep your eye on the centre line and you can drive to Auckland, no sweat, he would say. I looked out for the motorway signs to make sure we weren't lost. At the bottom of the hill, just before the city, I saw a truck full of lambs turn off the main road.

'Beautiful,' Dad said when we drove past the sea. 'Look at that water, bub. One day I'll teach you how to fish. Fresh fish from the sea. We can make our own fish and chips.'

I wondered how long it took us to get here. And how long it would take us to get back home. I didn't want fish I had to catch myself. I didn't want to follow the Ones and end up in Auckland. I wanted rump steak from a raffle ticket. Old songs under the blue plastic. Turtles. Doughnuts.

'We fished here all the time, your mum and me. Ages ago, before you came along.'

Mum loved the water and she taught me to swim. The hard way, in the sea, with no boards to help me float. The air in my body kept me from sinking. My arms and my legs got me moving. And soon I learned to breathe with the waves. I dived under the water without getting scared. It felt safe under the sea. Like a giant bubble. Like a pillow over your ears at night that kept away the bogeyman.

The last time I went to the beach with Mum we didn't paddle in the water or build castles in the sand. We sat on the rocks and said nothing for minutes.

We went through a tunnel. It felt like being under the sea. I forgot about Bluey. Then we got to the other side.

'Remember that time we walked through that tunnel, bro? Remember that night?'

'We were dumb kids back then.'

'Dumb kids back then, all right.'

We stopped at the lights. The buildings in the city made me feel tiny. Almost invisible.

'Remember that prick, bro? Big Al or something, they used to call him. Remember what he tried to do?'

Dad knew I wanted him to look at me and he didn't. I tried not to let my feelings get hurt.

'What a cunt, eh, bro? Remember what he did?'

Dad said nothing about Bluey using the C word. He said nothing until we got near the big cricket field in the city.

'Fuck's sake, you idiots! Get off the bloody road!'

Some kids came out of the cricket field. Dad stopped to let them cross. I thought he wasn't going to. Then I wondered 'bout this Big Al fulla, who he was.

'Chatting up your missus like that. Fuck that, eh, bro?'

Dad pressed the horn and the kids turned back and gave him the fingers. I wasn't expecting that and the corners of my mouth turned up without me making them.

'Stop that, Rosie!'

My face went warm again. *Whirr*. Stop. I stopped smiling.

'Served him right what happened to him, bro.'

I looked in the side mirror at Bluey. His lips went like string and his head shook from side to side. He was staring out the window. Remembering things.

'I never seen you so mad, bro,' he said.

My dad only got angry when he watched the rugby. And mainly at the ref who was usually a blind idiot. *Come on, ref – open your eyes! What's the matter with you? You blind idiot!* He hardly even swears in front of me. I learned most of my swear words from Nanny and Papa's place.

'I thought you were gonna give him the bash, bro. I had to hold you back, you remember?'

It went quiet in the car for a minute and I could tell Dad was talking in his head. He gawked at the road like he was watching a movie. I wanted to say something but I opened my window instead. *Whirr.*

'Rosie!' I jumped in my seat. 'Fuck's sake, girl. You gonna pay for that when it's broke?' Dad leaned over me and pushed down the button. The window wound back up. It was hard to breathe with his elbow in my tummy.

'Shut up, Rosie. Why are you crying?'

By the time I felt the tears at the back of my eyeballs, it was too late to stop them from falling out. I wiped them off my face with my sleeve. I sniffed only when I felt the snot dripping.

'You were pretty strong, bro, even back then when you was just a young fulla.' I caught Dad watching Bluey in his driver's mirror. 'Juju started screaming, remember? You had to calm her down. She went fucking mental.'

Bluey was talking to the window now as if it was gonna talk right back. Then he turned and looked straight at me in my side mirror.

When we passed the hospital I felt more tears behind my eyeballs. I opened and shut my eyelids quickly to keep the tears inside. Smoke was coming out of one of the hospital chimneys. *Where they burn the dead bodies*, my cousin had told me. My aunty heard her and gave her a clip around the taringa. Cos that was about the time my mum died.

'What a dumb cunt.'

I turned and made bung eyes at Bluey. He couldn't see me, but Dad could.

'Rosie.'

Apart from his lips, Dad's face was ice. Frozen. His knuckles stuck out like tiny rocks around the steering wheel.

'You were ready to smash that prick, bro. Who knows what would've happened if Juju hadn't screamed?'

The back of my neck started to itch again. When Mum died Dad screamed hard out like a baby. I never told him I heard him cos it's none of my business to know about things. But ever since then, I know grown men can break too.

'Bro,' said Dad, 'we're nearly there, bro.'

The old shops in Newtown looked like rundown shoe boxes. All sorts of wires crisscrossed above us.

'Serves that arsehole right what he got, bro.'

I still didn't know what time it was, but Nanny and Papa would be starting to worry.

'*Housie*, Dad.'

'Shut up, Rosie.'

I looked into my side mirror. I hated that stupid moon-eyed baby.

'Serves that fucker right. I didn't even care when they sent me off. I laughed in their fucking faces, I did.' Then Bluey laughed. He laughed and laughed and laughed and laughed.

We stopped at the lights and Dad turned to look at Bluey. 'Stop it, bro. My daughter's here.'

It went quiet in the car for a full minute it felt like. I kept my eyes up front.

'Sorry, bro. Sorry, Rosie. I forget where I am sometimes.'

Nobody said nothing the rest of the way.

At the end of the road we turned the corner and Dad parked up near the flats by the zoo. Even from here, I could hear the animals crying inside their cages.

Bluey got out and tapped my window. I pressed the button.

'Sorry 'bout the language, Rosie.' His face and dreadlocks took up the whole space. 'I'm not a brainy box like you are, Rosie. Just a dumb cunt is me.'

He tried to smile and I stared at the gap in his teeth. And then I remembered. 'Hey, Bluey,' I said, 'why they call you Bluey?'

His face went soft, like a baby's. 'It's my blue eyes, Rosie. My blue eyes.'

He disappeared into one of the flats. I watched Dad watch Bluey go.

Ugly

The steam on the mirror irons out her features. The edges of her nostrils melt into her cheeks. But her lips are swollen and crooked still. Hair shapeless, dull and arid. A dab of purple shadows her under-eye.

She strips down to her undies. The sores on her legs have stopped seeping. The scabs block the spillage, the hard little domes spotting her limbs. Sores take longer to heal when you leave them exposed, and plasters and Dettol belong in other people's cabinets. She dips her toes into the tepid bath water, then drags up a rope of knotted hair. It's snagged on a callus on the side of her foot, wispy and shimmering.

She flicks the hair across the floor and it lands in a mass by the sink. Then she looks back at the bath water, the ring of dirt and dead skin around the bath's edge, deposits left behind by her younger siblings. She's learned to ignore it. Being the oldest, there is no one left to rush for and at least she gets to bathe in silence.

She peels off her underwear, pulling the fabric away from her skin. She is careful not to disturb the fresh scab on her knee, regrowth after falling on it in the playground at school. Jamie Fletcher, the girl down the road, shoved her onto a six-studded Lego. It pierced her flesh, the pain pulsing through her leg, up her spine to her throat, where she swallowed it like puke. She was too self-conscious to spit it out, admit the hurt, bring attention to herself. And the gash that had started to heal bled again through her trousers like an inkblot. She didn't see a warped butterfly in that peculiar shape; she saw her mother's tired eyes and shoulders, slumped at her clumsiness and disregard for things they couldn't replace. She went to the girls' toilets to clean up, wiping the blood with the waxed toilet paper, and the scab dropped to the concrete floor.

Her mother always warned her about talking to outsiders. 'They fuss over nothing. You bring your problems home.'

Her problems were never her problems alone. They were family problems, burdens shared, as if the family walked the world as one. But the shame she felt of not fighting back, of letting that Fletcher girl put her down, made her step up to the school nurse that Friday. Drown one problem by creating another. Shun the spotlight by shining it somewhere else.

'Does anyone have any boo-boos to show me?'

They were too old for that kind of talk, but that's what the nurse called them – boo-boos. It made the other children giggle.

The girl lumbered to the front of the room, her ungainly feet filling the gaps on the mat. The covert glance the nurse shared with the teacher told the girl she was doing something extraordinary. She rolled up her trouser leg and let the cool air breathe over the broken skin. She felt it whip across her wounded kneecap and lap at the dried blood on her shin. She heard their muffled gasps. All she could do then was wish she could bury the cut inside herself where it could fester unseen.

Her underwear falls to the bathroom floor, gusset

browned from three days of wear. She used to own five pairs, but she soiled one at school, which she hid behind a cistern and Jamie found. The girl watched her chase the boys around the playground with them dangling at the end of a pencil. It thrilled the other children to be that disgusted, to catch glimpses of her sodden underwear flapping in the air. The boys raced through the playground squealing like rats. And when the other children, faces contorted, eyes and lips twisted into uneven lines, showed their disgust, she did the same. Laughing when they did. Pointing when they did. Mocking the owner of the underwear as they did.

She looks at the scars on her feet from older sores. Her whole body repulses her. It makes her want to peel away her skin like a mandarin, poke her thumbnail into her waist and slice it down the side of her body. Over her hip bones. The insides of her thighs where her flesh is most tender. Down, down, down. Over knees, calves, the balls of feet. Scars, calluses, broken sores. Expose flesh and tissue to the air. Pierce her veins with a dirty fingernail and let the blood drain onto the floor. She wants to lay in her blood and slide across the room. Feel her nakedness against the cold lino and throw her body against the bathtub. Let the pain leach out in tiny drips. Wrap her limbs around the pipe under the sink. Watch her veins shrivel up like worms in the sun.

Her toes curl on impact as the scum breaks around them, the bath water rippling around her ankle. When she is older she will learn how one tiny movement can alter the next, how a course can change or an expectation can be eroded. How something can become redundant or have new energy breathed into it. But for now, her feet touch the bottom of the tub and she flexes her toes in the grit. She makes shapes rather than patterns, giving the doodles a sense of completeness. The grit is nowhere near as thick as the sands in the ocean. She doesn't feel that sudden hollow beneath her feet as sand is sucked out by retreating waves. The grains here are stony crumbs, which only press into her skin or disintegrate beneath her weight.

When she sits, the water rests an inch above her waist and makes her shiver, but it doesn't sting, thanks to the crusted domes. She turns on the hot water and it plunges towards her feet. It makes gulping noises that bounce off the walls. She shifts until the grit moves around the edges of her buttocks, giving her a smooth surface to rest on. The hot water creeps its way along the bath and she settles into its warmth.

'Oi! Turn that hot water off.' The palm of her mother's hand slaps against the bathroom door. The handle flaps.

The girl grabs the facecloth from the small shelf in the wall. It has hardened into a misshapen ball. She knows there will be gunk in the corners of her siblings' eyes still, their fingers too uncoordinated to clear the nooks in their faces. She unfurls the stiffened cloth, dips it into the water, wraps her hand in it and feels the grime from weeks of scrubbing coat her palm and fingers. She turns off the tap, the thinning fabric barely protecting her hand from the heat. The door handle stops flapping.

'When was the last time you washed your hair?' When adults probed for answers, she was often ill-prepared. 'Your head is full of nits. So many kutu. Do you wash your hair with soap or just wet it with the water?'

The nurse is her mother's cousin. Soon other family members would know. The humiliation made her stomach ache and she stopped eating for three days. The nurse made partings in her hair, exposing the flock of lice and eggs.

'Maggots,' said Jamie, making sure the girl could hear. 'I heard they got maggots in their cupboards because the food in their house is stale and rotten.'

'And fleas,' the other children chipped in.

'And nits.'

'And *ghosts.*'

'They have to light candles because they have no power and they wash in the same bath water and eat the same porridge the whole week. It sits on their oven and the maggots crawl through it, and at night, the ghosts come down from the ceiling and piss in it.'

The ring of dirt around the bath has grown thicker. Floating by her foot is the plaster from the nurse and, next to it, the moistened facecloth. Her skin feels itchy and she scratches at the sore on her knee. It isn't long before blood is collecting under her fingernails.

The toilet door next to the bathroom creaks open. Through the walls she can hear rubber wheels squeaking along the lino, her mother's pride and joy. White with flecks of gold, pink roses with thornless vines. It makes her angry, the pretty, perfect lino with its thorns conveniently erased.

The hub from a wheel scrapes along the wall, making her body spasm with guilt. One of the wheels needs oil, which she was meant to borrow from her uncle after school. But the journey between school and home makes her heart race and it worries her mother whenever she's late.

'A stroke,' the nurse whispered to the teacher, 'one morning at home. They thought it was a heart attack but after tests they confirmed it – stroke. Paralysed on his left side. Not expected to walk again.'

The girl hums to drown out the bumps. She can hear the strain in her mother's voice. It's been a long day, another long day, like every day for the past seven months, and soon her mother will leave for work. She will depend on the girl to take care of her father. They are a wrestling duo, tapping in and out of the ring to be relieved, giving the other time to catch their breath. She tries not to think about her time in the ring.

'Is your dad dead?'

The girl carried on walking, making her way to the school gates. Jamie and her small gang followed her.

'Hey, ugly!' Jamie called out. 'I said, is your dad dead or something?'

The girl didn't know why Jamie's mother gave her a boy's name. Maybe she had a dick.

A stone hit the back of her head. It shocked her and she rubbed the area to alleviate the pain. She turned in time to see Jamie pelt another rock at her. It clipped her on the cheek, just under her eye.

The children gathered round, trapping her in a circle, more kids joining them to witness the slaughtering. Some of them sniggered behind their hands. Others laughed more openly, exposing their molars. She rubbed her cheek and considered the bruising. Another thing for her mother to worry about.

'Did ya hear me, ugly?' Jamie badgered. 'Are you deaf and stupid as well as ugly? I heard your dad is dead, eh. He dropped dead at work, right in the factory. My dad said. So don't try to lie to me, ugly. He used to work with him. He said your dad was useless. He probably deserved to die. Is he the ghost that pisses in your porridge?'

The children heckled her, chanting 'Ghost piss! Ghost piss!' The girl raised a shield only she could see. Not the sticks-and-stones carry-on her mother would lecture her about, but a wall to protect her like the crusted domes under her clothes. A veil that kept her safe.

Their constant chanting swirled in her brain. Their heads rolled back. Their laughing was so hard and loud it threatened to awaken the ghost that pissed in her porridge. Make it abandon the house and sweep across the street over houses and front yards to the school gate.

A swish of wind brushed the back of her neck and she turned in time to watch a shapeless mist descend upon them. Falling like fog, it drifted, creating a film that smudged out the children's faces. It felt like cooling rain to her, but the others around her screamed as if the droplets were acid.

Their laughter turned to cries. Their cries turned to screams as the mist swallowed them whole. But the mist had the opposite effect on the girl. She opened her mouth wide and took in large gulps, breathed it in and felt it freshen the back of her throat. It tasted like the mouthwash the dental nurse gave her to spit back out. It was the purest oxygen and it filled her with . . . she didn't have the word for it. She felt giddy. Through thin breaks in the fog she saw ulcers and sores develop on the skins of the other children. The wounds seeped blood and pus, the red and yolky fluid running down their limbs. Mucus leaked from their nostrils, dripping over their lips, drying on their faces in thin tracks. Tears rolled down their cheeks. Saliva hung from their teeth. Their bodies squirmed like dying flies on a windowsill.

'What are you gonna do now, ugly?'

The girl recognised the desperate voice.

'This is your fault, you ugly freak show!'

The girl was voiceless as the angry girl hovering above her contorted in the mist. She could barely make out Jamie's form, her body now covered in jagged barnacles. Her pale skin was smeared in blood and pus and spew, and from her mouth crawled thousands of maggots.

Joy. That's the word she was looking for. This was what it felt like.

It took her minutes to pull herself away, and when she finally did, her step was lighter, though her feet dragged along the footpath like dead weight. She barely noticed the throbbing around her eye, the extra rips in her T-shirt, the new cut on her upper lip. The whiplash. Her shins and elbows were bleeding, but the fresh scrapes were invisible to her for now.

In the bath, she soaps her elbows gently, massaging the skin with her fingertips. The toilet flushes in the room next door. The hub of the wheelchair scratches along the wall.

Sisters

Aunty Esther and her tribe arrive first thing on Tuesday morning.

'Hullo, my darling.' She smothers me at the front door and I'm sucked into her embrace, clamped tight against her chest, her cushiony arms wrapped round my back. The scent of the coconut oil in her hair makes me gasp. Then she holds me at arm's length to get a better look. 'Big day on Friday,' she says, meaning my birthday. I've been trying to forget it.

Her children push past us and race down the corridor.

'Kura! Tevita! Ngatokorua! No'oputa! Tua!' she calls. 'Come give your cousin a kiss.'

I'm relieved when they don't. Their howling threatens to stir the spirits of loved ones, whose faces, trapped inside framed sepia photographs, line the corridor walls. My cousins treat the hallway like an afternoon at the track. Finally, they dump their bags and blankets in one of the vacant bedrooms.

Uncle Tiare follows Aunty Esther into the house, first greeting Mum in the sitting room. He catches her up on the progress of his avocado tree, filling the space in the room with his presence. 'E, reka!' he boasts. 'Everybody laughed at me, sis.'

Mum and Uncle are close like siblings. He's been part of the family long before he married my aunt, way back when they were kids with no shoes, running through my papa's taro plantation in Rarotonga. 'They said I was a foolish man to grow an avocado tree up there in South Auckland.' He's grinning. 'But two avocados I got this year, sis!' He holds up two fingers in front of Mum's face. 'Two whole bloody avocados!'

Aunty Esther shushes her husband out of the room, telling him what a foolish man he is to boast about such trivial things.

'Two whole bloody avocados,' she mocks. 'And it only took you ten bloody years!'

Mum lets Uncle brush her cheek with a kiss before he weaves his way through the house to the back door and out into the backyard, reuniting briefly with other rellies along the way.

'Two whole bloody avocados,' we hear him say.

Aunty Teina comes next.

'Auē,' she cries, seeing how much I've grown since her last visit. She fixes her lipstick after branding my cheek with a kiss. Her lips are fuller and plumper than I remember. She beckons me to her, letting me sink into her arms like they're an old, familiar La-Z-Boy. The scent of her perfume fills my head with pictures of places and people she's known – French waiters in Paris, flamenco dancers in Seville, nuns in Rome who strut the cobblestone footpaths of the Vatican City in twos and threes.

There are no restless children hanging off her designer dress knock-off – an outfit that is worlds away from the hand-me-down pants and shirts from her cousins that she grew up in when she was a boy back in the islands. And it pleases me to get to share my room with her over all my other aunts. When she teases me with her usual questions, I never feel picked on, like my cousins do. But the awkwardness is still there.

'You got a boyfriend yet?' she asks in her serious voice. 'You're old enough now,' she says with a wink.

That's not true, if she means what I think she means. My cheeks flare and my tongue fishes inside my mouth, feeling for words. Aunty's eyes sparkle and when she pulls me back in for another embrace I hug her back with everything I've got.

By the afternoon, when Aunty Selina gets here, we already have a full house. But that's never stopped Mum's sisters from inviting themselves over.

'Let me look at you, my beautiful goddaughter,' Aunty Selina cries. She holds me to her bosom and soaks my hair with tears. I panic over the halo of frizz it will make. It's all right for some people – like Tuakana, whose hair is worthy of an American shampoo commercial. People like my cousin don't worry if their aunties cry into their hair. When I was still young enough to let my mum brush my hair, it would take her thirty minutes just to comb out the knots. Several spokes would snap off the plastic comb as she raked it through, and to save on tears – both of ours – she'd sweep my hair back into a single ponytail to keep the creeping tumbleweed out of my eyes.

I recognise the little gold crucifix that rests between my aunty's collarbones. She gave me the same necklace on the day of my First Holy Communion. That was over seven years ago now.

'Now we're truly mother and daughter in Christ,' she'd said. 'As long as you're wearing that chain close to your heart, we'll always be seen like that in the eyes of God.'

Caught up in that day's celebrations, I lost the necklace somewhere between the first reading and the prayers of the faithful. Mum got upset with me, embarrassed by my clumsy ways. My First Holy Communion meant a lot to her.

Uncle Craig, Aunty Selina's husband, carries into the house the rest of her first-class baggage. I notice the final stages of sunburn in his face, his pale skin shedding like a gecko's. Aunty steps towards me again and swallows me in her arms. She smells like tea-tree oil and feijoa.

*

When Mum was fifteen, she sailed alone to New Zealand on a ship called the *White Magnolia*. She didn't know it then, but she'd never dig her toes into the sands of Muri Beach again. Saying goodbye would become a slow-rending heartbreak. Ngatangiia, the eastside district on the island of Rarotonga where she grew up, would become distant, like a paradise in novels written by white men with brown wives and a longing to escape the rat race.

Her loneliness in those early days was eased by the wild magnolia bush that grew outside her bedroom window. It was the first time she'd seen the flower that shared its name with the ship that brought her here. It was unlike the hibiscus and frangipani blooms she'd known from her childhood, and she welcomed its strangeness. She craved unfamiliarity. The more peculiar and foreign her surroundings, the easier it became to forget what she'd come from.

The bedroom she rented in a boarding house in Newtown was furnished with a single bed and a set of bedside drawers that remained empty. She kept her clothes – three homemade dresses, two pairs of shoes, some underwear and a secondhand winter coat – neatly folded inside her cracked leather suitcase on the polished wooden floor.

Another girl from her village helped her find work in a factory in the city. She sewed zippers onto men's trousers and later she made uniforms for the military. The factory was cold and mechanical, an artificial space where young women like her communed. In the city there were no lanky coconut trees to climb, no mangoes to pick in summer, and the sea was too open to strangers to dive for seafood. Her life became a series of clocking in and out with time cards and eating mackerel drowned in coconut cream hacked out of tin cans.

In the evenings, she'd watch the leaves from the tī kōuka flap in the wind outside her bedroom window and the red needles from the pōhutukawa tree fall like tiny spindles. The magnolia bush remained unwavering. In that bedroom, alone at night, she would sew a green-and-white tīvaevae. The oversized petals on that bedspread were an ode to those alien flowers.

When Mum sailed to New Zealand on that giant, steel vaka, she didn't know that she'd never see her parents again. And it wasn't until years later, when she'd saved enough money for her sisters to come too, that she started to call this place home.

*

The sisters are gathered in the sitting room with the other women in the family. After the evening prayers are said, they form a ring on the mat, cross-legged on the floor with tīvaevae and continental blankets draped over their laps. Bags of freshly clipped chrysanthemums are emptied onto the floor and old newspapers laid out in the centre of the coven to catch the discarded greenery.

'That's what you are,' Dad used to tease Mum about my aunts. 'A coven of witches, like the disciples of the anti-Christ.'

That made Mum the high priestess.

Aunty Teina separates the flowers. She draws attention to her manicured hands: the polish on her fingernails painted by the masters; her skin, she would say, massaged by the beating wings of angels. She sorts the flowers by size before the women begin weaving them into garlands.

Mum is centre stage. She looks radiant surrounded by her women, their raucous banter rising to the ceiling.

'Eh, sister,' says one of Mum's cousins, 'remember back home, when we were still girls? Remember how we used to make all the beautiful 'ei to catch the boys' eyes?' The women screech like a bat colony. I look over at Mum. Her face is serene like she's dreaming about the olden days. 'You used to catch a few eyes, eh, sis?' her cousin goes on. 'You could've had any boy in that backward village.'

Aunty Teina pipes up. 'But she wasn't a cheeky girl like you, cousin.' Again the women shriek, slapping their thighs as they thread more flowers. 'She didn't show off her beautiful 'ei like they were going out of fashion.'

'Oh but, sis,' another cousin says as the first dissolves into the wallpaper, 'you remember when we first came out? You remember living in Newtown? You remember that boarding house we stayed in?' I finetune my hearing like I'm dialling in on a secret radio station. 'You remember how we snuck out at night to smoke by that ugly bush out the back?' I raise my eyes at Mum. She'd banned cigarettes from the house like they were weed. 'Remember how we dug that little hole in the ground to bury our butts in so we wouldn't get caught?' The room fills with high-pitched cackles. Mum says nothing, just smiles her Mona Lisa smile.

One by one the room fills with the beautiful garlands. The scent is overpowering. I help some of the aunties carry the flowers into the bathroom and hang the garlands from a dismantled broom handle balanced atop the shower curtain rail. When we return to the sitting room, the old newspapers and discarded greenery are disposed of and the women have settled in for a game of euchre.

'Eh, sis,' Aunty Esther accuses Mum in Cook Islands Māori. 'What's with all the bad luck in your house? How come none of us can pick up this card? What kind of curse have you put on your sisters? Why are you cheating with your black magic?'

Aunty Selina's eyes are downcast. She is silent amongst the din. It's her turn to turn down the gold-headed Jack; instead, she fingers the corner of her middle card and pauses to make sure everybody knows what that means.

'*Ooo*,' Aunty Teina jeers, her voice rising.

Aunty Selina, now satisfied, withdraws the card from her hand. She returns it to the rest of the deck – placing it facedown to torture the other players – and grips the handsome Jack with the tips of her fingers, bringing him back to rest against her crucifix.

'I wouldn't put that devil card so close to my chest if I was you,' Aunty Esther says. 'Not even Jesus can save you from that sunstruck-headed demon.'

I'm glad Uncle Craig isn't in the room to hear that. The freckles on his cheeks would have blended like one giant sunspot.

The other women mute their laughter, their eyes bulging. They're careful not to pick sides, but more from fear of backing the wrong sibling – the less clever sibling, the one most likely to lose – than from keeping the family peace.

It's well after midnight before the laughter in the sitting room dies down. From my bedroom I can hear the final visitors leave and the door to my parents' bedroom open and close. Aunty Selina and Uncle Craig will sleep in the sitting room this first night.

'Make sure no funny business in here,' I hear Aunty Teina say in her amplifying voice. No chance of that. Two other aunties and four cousins are also destined for that sitting-room floor. I imagine her eyeballing Uncle Craig, anyway, as they set up the foam mattresses.

Later, when Aunty Teina tiptoes into my room and slips into her nightie in the dark, I keep my eyes shut and let her inspect me. When I hear her speak in whispers, the words sliding from her mouth in one breath, I stop myself in time from answering her back. She is praying over me. It startles me. The earnestness in her voice is unnerving. But before long, her soft chanting lulls me off to sleep, and that night I dream in Polaroids.

On the Wednesday, the men are sent out on errands. Dad takes me with him to get me out of the house.

'Make sure the hall is big enough, eh. I don't want nobody to say our family is mean. Remember what happened to Nina and her lot? People say they make their guests stand out in the rain because they too cheap to hire a hall. You want that to happen to us? The shame.'

'Make sure you pick out some nice, fat pigs. I don't want people to say we too cheap to feed them. And when you order the fish, make sure it's fresh, caught that day and still flapping.'

'And when they come back,' I hear another of the aunties

say as we flee the house, 'they can mow the lawns and clean out the garage. We need space for the marquee, and they're not drinking their beer in my sister's house.'

The men know better than to argue with the aunties. They pile into their cars, armed with the morning's instructions, Dad leading the convoy in his Holden sedan. Uncle Tiare is beside him. I'm in the back seat.

The drive home is bumpier than a flight into Wellington. The three piglets are stuffed into sacks, their squirming young bodies thrown into the boot. Little hooves press into my spine through the fabric of the back seat as the piglets try to kick their way free from their burlap prisons. Blinded and bagged, their desperate squealing pierces my eardrums. I imagine the sweat running down the side of my face is a droplet of blood.

I hold my voice back, not wanting to add more drama to the day, not wanting to cause more pain. The trapped animals continue to claw at my back through the membrane of vinyl that separates us. I sit as far forward on my seat as I can, trying to trick my brain into happier places.

'Ana,' Dad calls out from the driver's seat, peering at me through the rear-view mirror. 'You all right, girl?'

Uncle Tiare turns in his seat. 'Gee, girl, you soft or something? How else do you think we're gonna eat? We can't just live on potato salad.'

The men laugh, but Dad winks at me through the mirror.

'Kiwi girls,' Uncle Tiare teases, rolling his eyes at Dad. 'Not like proper island girls.'

At home I follow Dad and Uncle round the back of the house. Uncle carries one of the piglets still trapped in its sack while Dad carries the other two, one wriggling bag tucked under each armpit. A table made from old beer crates and a plank of wood found at the tip have been erected along the back fence to prep the meat for the umu.

'Go inside,' says Dad. I look down at the sacked piglets twitching on the makeshift table. 'It's okay. Go. Help Aunty Teina in the kitchen.'

Aunty Teina is buttering cabin bread biscuits. The lids of tinned corned beef are peeled back and the marbled meat is being scooped onto plates. Bowls of quartered tomatoes from the next-door-neighbour's garden and chunks of boiled taro soaking in warmed-up coconut cream are placed on the kitchen table. I slice some bread, stacking the pieces high on a dinner plate, making two spongy towers that lean to one side. I'm focused on steadying the bread, sweeping the crumbs off the Formica tabletop, when I hear the high-pitched shrieks from the backyard.

I race to the back door and open it in time to see the blood gush from one of the piglets onto the grass. I struggle to breathe, gasping for air, just as Dad turns round to catch my eye. Blood drips from the knife in his hand. I can't move so I wait for the reprimand. Instead, Dad turns his back to me and Aunty Teina gently pulls me into the house.

There are chores for Africa, as Aunty Teina would say, and I'm grateful for it. All this hustle and bustle will take my mind off the days ahead.

'Aunty,' Aileen calls out to Mum in the next room. Kitchen drawers and cupboards fly open as she whips past them like a tempest. I can hear the other women in the sitting room keeping Mum occupied. 'Where do you keep your potato peeler, Aunty?' I pull open the cutlery drawer and dig out the peeler. She takes it from me, flicking her head in thanks. We sit down at the kitchen table, pages of old newspapers spread out to catch the potato skins.

'Better make plenty spuds,' Aunty Teina orders, as if we're making potatoes from scratch. 'We're expecting another big crowd tonight.' A ribbon of potato skin unfurls from my knife. I hold my breath to steady my knife's movements, determined to shave the whole spud in one seamless peel. When the potato skin snaps, I exhale and swallow the air with urgency.

It was Dad's idea to celebrate my birthday. 'Your family's coming from all over,' he said. 'Uncle Tiare and Aunty Esther and their lot. Your Aunty Mi'i and her lot from Sydney.' Two buses from Auckland will trundle down on Thursday night, and family members have been billeted out like orphaned schoolchildren. Ever since I can remember I've felt like I'm being fussed over. Treated like something breakable – precious and rare and too delicate to hold. An oddity. The special child. The one not meant to be.

When Mum found out she was pregnant, it followed years of trying.

'We tried everything,' Mum told me. 'Even some of the old ways from home.'

'Voodoo magic,' Dad teased.

'I just learned to live with it, the thought of having no child of my own. It wasn't God's will. Not in the cards.'

When Aunty Esther got pregnant, Mum said she was happy for her. But it was hard for her to watch her younger sister fall pregnant again and again. Aunty even offered Mum one of her children to love, but Mum said she couldn't, and she loved them anyway.

Then she got pregnant.

'Oh,' Mum said. 'That day was my second happiest. I was more happy then than when I first met your father—'

'That was your Uncle Taki's fault,' Dad said. 'He dragged

me along to that dance in Newtown. I'd just broken up with the love of my life,' he'd tease, making sure Mum could hear. 'My old girlfriend from up the Naki – we'd been together since school days. And your Uncle Taki, he thought it was a good idea for me to meet some other ladies. Take my mind off things. "Island girls aren't like your Papa'a girls," your Uncle Taki would say. And, man oh man, was he right!' Dad laughed. 'Your mother is out of this world. And then when your aunties arrived—'

And that's when Mum jumped in.

'And the happiest day of my life,' she'd say, 'was the day I first held you.'

The day I was born, Dad planted a magnolia shrub in one corner of the backyard. My placenta is buried deep beneath its roots. The roots took their time to take hold. Mum said it was because the plant was like me, taking its time to get ready for living. The seasons passed many times over before the florets started to bloom, so for years that plant hung naked and limp like a ragdoll.

For years I resented Mum for choosing that plant to remember my birth. Not a rose bush. Not a lemon tree. Not a native shrub of some sort. But a Frankenstein of a flower – a freak of nature. And Mum loved that plant, despite its strangeness, its slowness. Then, the year its flowers finally started to bloom, Mum found out about the cancer, and I hated that plant more. I despised its hideous flowers. They were garish and obtrusive, and it broke me to know that something so unwanted would get to live on when other things more cherished would not.

'May as well get the practice in now, cuz,' Aileen says across the table from me. 'We got that mountain of mainese to make for Friday.'

We peel two large pots of spuds for the mainese, then chop four large cans of sliced beetroot. I'm pleased we don't live in the olden days, when Mum cooked and peeled the beetroot from raw, the ruby-coloured juices running between her fingers as she sliced through its flesh with a serrated bread knife. That's how we cook the carrots still, from fresh, but the peas come frozen out of a plastic bag.

Mum taught me how to make the potato salad years ago, a recipe passed down over generations from her mother's side. The secret to the perfect mainese, she said, was in how you made the dressing. 'Don't rush with the dressing, baby. Add the oil to the egg yolks bit by bit.'

That was Mum's mantra: be patient, slow down, don't rush yourself, there's time.

The eggs are cracked on the edge of the kitchen bench and the yolks pulled away from the whites. Be patient, slow down, don't rush yourself, there's time.

As I dribble the oil into the bowl, the humming whisks from the electric beater churn the oil and egg yolks into dressing.

'We didn't have electric beaters back in the day,' Mum said. 'We used to beat the dressing by hand, with a whisk your Mama Ruau kept in a cardboard box. It was one of her prized possessions, that whisk. The true secret weapon to her mainese dressing.'

I can't imagine a kitchen tool being anyone's prized possession, unless it was studded with black pearls and granted its owner three wishes.

By five thirty in the evening more rellies have arrived. The younger cousins are a sea of faces bobbing around Mum like waves in the sitting room. She is flanked by Aunty Esther and Aunty Selina, who sit cross-legged on the floor. Aunty Teina is in the kitchen keeping an eye on the food. Flowers gifted by those who can't be here are arranged in vases and plastic buckets. They decorate the room, dwarfed only by the magnolia blooms picked that morning. Mum's green-and-white tīvaevae, folded down to the size of a cushion, lies beneath a framed photograph of her. The bedspread and the photograph are placed at the foot of her coffin. I sit beside the couch at Dad's feet.

Once the sitting room is full, the corridor and kitchen start to hum with more visitors, the chatter filling each corner of the house. When Father O'Shea arrives to lead the Rosary, the people part like the Red Sea. He occupies the chair next to Mum, acknowledging her first, then me and Dad, then he says a 'Kia orana' to everyone else.

'Evening, Father,' Uncle Tiare calls out from the corridor. 'We've been practising our singing for you tonight, Father.' The rellies shuffle awkwardly in their seats. Tonight's singing practice was a string of ultimatums of what songs to sing, by whom and at what volume.

'That's most excellent, Tiare,' says Father O'Shea. 'I'm looking forward to some beautiful singing tonight, then.'

Aunty Esther gives her husband the look. He can thank God later that Father's in the house.

'And do we have people to say the decades of the Rosary tonight?' Father asks.

'Yes, Father,' Dad says, rubbing my shoulder. 'Ana is going to start.' I expose too many of my teeth and gums and hope I've remembered enough of the words. When Father smiles but says nothing, I try not to read into it.

The strumming of a guitar opens the Rosary, and Aunty Esther leads us with the evening's first hymn. Her voice cuts through the air like a whistling conch shell, which encourages the other oldies to drown her out. Soon the house is heaving with over-earnest singing, the words slowed down to magnify the gravity. The cousins whose parents are responsible hang their heads, avoiding eye contact. Only Aunty Teina, with no children of her own to shame, holds back. When it's my turn to recite the Lord's Prayer, I speak the words as fast as I think I can get away with. I've memorised them to perfection. The oldies reply in united slow-motion: 'Holy Mary Mother of *Goooooooooooood* . . .'

After the final hymn, each part of the song performed as agreed, the action moves to the kitchen. Orders are given above the clattering of plates and cutlery, and I'm swept along on my cousins' zeal. Back in my bedroom, every inch of space is filled with teenage bodies and voices.

'Hey, cuz,' Tuakana says, reaching into her tote bag. I can smell her apple shampoo. 'Help me do my hair, K?' She holds up an electric crimping iron. It dumbfounds me, the thought of deliberately making your hair like mine. My other cousins are sprawled all over the floor. This is what it feels like to have sisters.

'You want?' Tuakana asks.

'Don't need it,' I say.

'Lucky,' she says, and I read her face for irony. When I'm sure there isn't any, I watch in silence as the cousins take turns.

'How you doing tonight, cuz?' Tuakana asks.

I shrug. My struggle to find words has only gotten worse.

When one of the Auckland cousins bursts into the room screaming, I feel relief.

'Cuz,' she shrieks, looking at me.

'Cuz?' I say.

'Got my . . . *you know* . . .'

I don't know. I look over at Tuakana, feeling like a toddler.

The Auckland cousin tugs at her skirt, pulling it as far from her body as she can. 'Got any plugs, cuz? I didn't bring nothin', cuz.'

'Oh.' The blood rushes to my face.

'Hang on, cuz,' says Tuakana. She digs in her bag and pulls out a box of tampons. She chucks it across the room at her, but it lands in my lap.

'Bloody nuisance, eh, cuz,' says the cousin in the doorway.

I throw the box over to her. 'Yeah, cuz.'

She takes the box and disappears down the corridor and into the bathroom.

Mum and I had the talk a few years ago, not long after I started Form One. I know it disappointed her that my sheets stayed as white as the day she'd cleaned them, but there was no hurrying Mother Nature. It just wasn't my time. When my friends started their periods, they'd tell me about the spotting in their underwear and the cramps, and how to place the sanitary pad into the inside of their panties, being careful to position it directly over the gusset to stop the blood from seeping out onto their clothes. Extra care was needed at school. You didn't want to be the girl with the blood patch on your uniform.

'But it does anyway,' said Sonia, my best mate. 'It leaks out the sides and stains your undies anyway. Or it gets on your uniform and your mum makes you wash it by hand. Because if I'm old enough to have babies, she says, then I'm old enough to clean my own bloody clothes.'

I've never had to clean my own bloody clothes.

On the Thursday, I help Aunty Esther pick more chrysanthemums. We ignore the magnolia bush in the other corner.

Because I know Aunty is judging my choice of flowers, I'm careful to choose only the ones with petals of a certain size – not so big that the 'ei katu will look like a floral bush is growing from the wearer's skull, but not so small that it can only be seen through the eyes of the Holy Spirit. In the sitting room, the aunties prepare to make more garlands for tomorrow, trimming leaves of flax and cutting them down to size to fit the various heads.

As we hover around the chrysanthemum bush, I hear Dad and the uncles prepping the pigs behind us. The pigs hang off three metal bars of the clothesline, carefully spaced out to balance the weight. The blood has stopped dripping from their throats, but the grass is stained red where it's seeped into the dirt.

'Reckon we deserve a little something after this hard work, eh, brother,' Uncle Tiare calls out to Dad. 'Some light refreshments, I reckon, my brother. I'm starting to feel a bit thirsty over here.'

Aunty Esther swivels on her heel, snapping her head into her shoulder.

'You men aren't here to drink,' she says, the open blades of the kitchen scissors in her hand. 'What do you think this place is? The Top Tavern? *Auē.*'

The men shuffle on the spot, eyes down, lips shut. When cousin Jack arrives with the clinking flagons in the wooden crates, they take a small step away from Uncle Tiare.

'*Auē,*' Aunty cries, blessing herself with the sign of the cross. '*Auē. Auē.* You men will pay for this. In the burning fires of Hell,' she says. 'Drinking in my sister's house' – she pauses to eyeball her husband – 'the night before we lay her to rest!'

It wasn't easy convincing Father to let us break protocol and keep Mum at home on her final night. But the aunties are unstoppable once they've made up their minds, and we all agreed – the Aunties, Dad and I – to keep her at home. No number of Hail Marys was going to help Father with this one.

Everybody knows the drill by now. The food is prepped. The rooms are cleaned. The floors are vacuumed and mopped and dried. The ornaments and picture frames are dusted and wiped. The good plates are brought out from the cabinet in the sitting room. They're washed and dried for the elders and Father. The everyday plates for everyone else are stacked on a bench in the kitchen. Paper plates on standby. Same with the cups – good cups, everyday cups, paper cups if needed. Who's saying what prayers is decided on. Hymns are chosen and there's one quick practice. And then we wait.

Father arrives. Rosary is said. Songs are sung. Copious amounts of food are eaten. Most of the adults retreat to the garage. Then begins the drinking.

'Bring that wine over here.' Aunty Esther waves her empty glass in the air. Uncle Tiare is quick to oblige. He presses down on the plastic tap sticking out from the cardboard box. The glass fills slowly to the brim with rose-coloured booze. He fills his own glass with more beer and the two of them swig their drinks as they sing along to the strumming ukulele. Another aunty beats an old cabin-bread biscuit tin with the palm of her hand. An older cousin taps a pair of spoons on his leg, which bounces to the rhythm of his foot as it taps the concrete floor. The garage is filled with spontaneous singing, the harmonies rich and unselfconscious.

I sit in one corner of the garage with Aunty Teina, where she's keeping me entertained with more stories from the olden days.

'Your Aunty Selina,' she whispers, 'she used to *hate* your

mother.' She laughs. I'm shocked at the reveal, eyeballing Aunty Selina by the garage door. She'd sworn off alcohol since meeting Uncle Craig, so the two of them sit po-faced and silent. 'She was so jealous of your mother because your mother was the pretty one. Your mother was the smart one. The chosen one. Like *you*,' she slurs, nudging me in the side with her elbow. 'Your mother was the first in the family to leave the island. The first to work in a Papa'a job. In a factory in the city, not some plantation like the rest of us commoners.' Her laugh turns into a cackle. It delights me. 'And when she met your father,' Aunty says, her voice now lower and deeper than normal, '*auē*, your aunty was *livid*. Absolutely livid.'

I look over at Dad, who's sitting amongst the musicians with their cobbled-together instruments. He's hidden behind half-drunk flagons piled on the table in front of him and I can hardly see his face.

'A Papa'a man,' Aunty laughs. 'That's the first thing your Mama Ruau said when she got your Mum's letter. "My daughter is going to marry a Papa'a man." Like your Dad was the King of England.'

Dad catches my eye. When he winks at me and the sides of his face crinkle when he smiles, I can see how Mum fell in love with him. How she let this man free her from that lonely boarding house. Even though he danced the two-step shuffle and sunburned too easily when they fished on the harbour.

'And then you came along,' Aunty says with a grin, 'and your aunty went *crazy* with the envy.'

I know Aunty Selina couldn't have children of her own. 'It's just one of those things,' Mum said.

'But you saved your aunty from herself,' Aunty Teina

goes on to say. 'The day she became your godmother was the happiest day of her life. There was no reason to be jealous of your mother anymore, because she too had the most precious thing your mum would ever have.'

I remember the gold crucifix I'd lost that day, with my careless ways and my thoughtlessness. I hadn't realised just how much my First Holy Communion had meant to my aunt.

'Auē!' Aunty Esther calls out from the other side of the garage. The shattering sounds of glass breaking takes over the singing. I look over at the musicians' table and see Dad holding his hand to his chest. The blood stain on his T-shirt from the cut spreads into a blot.

'Dad?' I rush over to him.

'It's okay, baby.' He tries to smile but the crinkles on the sides of his face have shifted to his forehead. He pulls the lower half of his T-shirt over his cut hand and hurries out of the garage. Drops of blood trickle onto the grass, mingling with the blood of the dead piglets. He makes his way across the lawn and back into the house. I follow him into the bathroom.

'It's just a little cut, baby,' he says. 'Just help me with the Band-Aid.' I help him strip off his T-shirt, which he uses to wrap his hand. 'Good thing your mum's not here to tell me off 'bout this,' he says, gesturing to the blood-stained top, trying to make me laugh.

I open the medicine cabinet and rummage for the plasters. Half-used containers of moisturisers and hand creams remind me Mum's not here to tell Dad off. Her small plastic bottle of coconut oil, an elixir for all ailments, sits in the back corner of the cupboard. Her toothbrush. Her tweezers. Her roll-on deodorant. Her nail clippers. Her sanitary pads. Her cotton balls and cotton buds. Her bobby pins. Her plastic comb. Her painkillers.

So many leftover painkillers.

'Baby?'

Dad puts one hand on my shoulder, which starts to shake with no volition. The tears fall from my eyes, blurring my sight so that when I turn round and collapse into my father's chest, all I can see is the blood-stained T-shirt wrapped round his cut hand. I hold my breath and contract my stomach muscles to keep the tears from falling but it only hurts more. In my gut and in my chest. I weep and my weeping turns into sobbing. The crying is hollow and deep and the echo of it bounces off the bathroom walls.

'Let it out, baby,' Dad says. His voice sounds like a lullaby.

I raise my head, the tears still clouding my eyesight, and catch the hazy outline of my mother's sisters in the doorway.

The aunties and I sleep in the sitting room that evening, our last evening with Mum before we bury her. Dad agrees to let us have the final night on our own. He jokes, 'All you women do is gossip, anyway.'

Aunty Teina and I lie on either side of Mum on the floor, our foam mattresses pushed up against her coffin. Some of the aunties and uncles are still in the garage, their drunken singing faint from the sitting room. I can hear the bustling in the kitchen from the other women preparing food for tomorrow.

'Sister,' Aunty Teina says, still drunk from the boxed wine. She leans over Mum, whose face looks more sunken than the previous nights. Her cheekbones are more pronounced. The colour is draining from her face. 'We're gonna make you proud, my sister,' she says. 'We made all your favourite recipes. Pineapple pie. Doughnuts. Pōke. Raw fish.' Her voice starts to crack. 'And you'd be proud of your girl, sister. She made the best mainese I've ever tasted. E reka!' She kisses her pinched fingers. 'Don't worry 'bout your girl, sister,' she says. 'I reckon she's tough as nuts.'

Mum's face has the gaunt look of a dead body days old. And the longer I look at it the more ugly it becomes. Like those magnolia flowers growing in the backyard and the ones in vases at the foot of her coffin. I hate those flowers and I hate her face. This isn't how I want to remember her.

Aunty Esther's tribe wakes first on the Friday.

'Kura! Tevita! Ngatokorua! 'No'oputa! Tua!' she says. 'Get up – get ready! I don't want us to be late!' I hear my cousins racing through the house.

'Darling,' Aunty Teina says from across the room. 'How are you feeling, my love?'

After last night I expect things to be different. I look into Mum's coffin but her face is sunken and dull again.

'Won't be long now, darling,' Aunty Teina reassures me. 'The day will be over before you know it. Then you can rest.'

Dad comes into the sitting room. He leans over Mum and kisses her on the cheek, whispering in her ear. I don't hear what he says. He reaches over and gives me a hug, his cut hand dressed with a fresh plaster.

When the lid of the coffin is shut and sealed, the long wail from the aunties stabs my ears like a silver needle. We drape Mum's coffin with the green-and-white tīvaevae and layer on top of that bunches of white magnolias. The framed photograph of Mum lies at the foot of her coffin.

I ride to the church in the hearse with Dad. When I

look behind us at Mum's closed casket, the smile in her photograph is how I will remember her. It's how I saw her last night in the sitting room when the low thrumming woke me from my sleep.

*

It was the faint scent of the magnolia blossoms that I noticed first. In my mind I pictured the stalks erect and luminous, droplets of dew on delicate petals. My eyes adjusted to the semi-darkness in the sitting room. The quivering flames from the tealight candles filled the space around Mum's open casket with a warm glow. It cast a gentle light over the white magnolias placed with care on either side of her. They looked as fresh as if they'd just been picked.

They were unrecognisable, my aunts. Their breasts and bellies were swollen. Their incantations were low, and I knew that I was one of only a few who could hear them. I felt timid in their nakedness, and when they beckoned me to join them, I shied away.

'Come,' said Aunty Teina. 'Don't be afraid.'

I felt drawn to the circle, my feet pulling me towards them. I looked closer into Mum's casket. The upward curves of her lips seemed more prominent now than in the days before. Aunty Teina tugged at my nightdress, pulling it up over my neck and shoulders, discarding my underwear next until I stood nude in front of them.

'Trust us,' said Aunty, her lips motionless.

I looked down at my feet, ashamed to see myself in their eyes. And in the flickering candlelight, I noticed a trickle of blood trail slowly down my inner thigh.

'Good,' said Aunty Esther, 'she's almost ready.'

Disoriented, I fumbled for my nightdress. Something blocked my movements and I floundered backwards, falling onto one of the mattresses in a clumsy heap. The blood stain on the sheet from my period spread into a blot. Instinctively, I shoved my hand between my legs to stop the bleeding. When I felt the wetness, I panicked. I held my hand in front of me and in the soft candlelight saw the blood on my fingers.

A transparent image of Mum came into view from the foot of my mattress. My mind began to turn over. She glowed in the dark like divinity, her lips forever pursed into that distinctive smile. Somewhere in the back of my mind my aunts recommenced their chanting.

'Mum?' I said. My own lips were still and I heard only the dull chorus of the aunties.

'Don't be afraid, my darling. Your time has come.'

I stared at the ghostly figure, longing to reach out to it.

'What do you mean? Mum? What's happening? What do you mean my time has come?' I felt tears on my cheeks. In my confusion, I forgot to tell Mum all the things I wanted to say. About the mainese I'd made. About the readings I did for the rosaries. How I'd helped Dad like I promised I would. If I could have that time again, that's what I'd do. I'd tell her those things. I'd reach over and touch her face, feel her warmth against me.

'You're ready, darling. Don't be afraid.'

The image of Mum dissipated like a sheet of ice in the sun. The aunts' chanting grew louder and louder. The words were alien but consoling. I joined the circle and let the same words fall from my mouth.

*

The day we bury Mum, I turn fifteen. I stand shoulder to shoulder with her sisters as we watch the men lower her coffin into the grave. The mat of artificial turf conceals the mounds of dirt that we will later use to bury her body. It feels natural to do so, to commit her body to the earth – like my placenta that's buried beneath that magnolia bush, beside the umu pit where we cooked today's feast, those piglets that hung lifeless from our clothesline for days.

Snatches of the green-and-white tīvaevae peek out from beneath the magnolias on top of the casket. The flower patterns so carefully patched into that tīvaevae used to prompt pity from the other women who sewed, the indistinct petals mistaken for deformed hibiscuses. As Father O'Shea scatters the first trowel of dirt over the coffin, I move beside Dad to tip the first handful of dirt into the grave.

'Ashes to ashes, dust to dust . . .' Father says.

I feel each grain of dirt as it slips between my fingers, and watch as the dirt falls into the hole in the ground. The wailing from my aunts sounds like television static, a constant hum that my ears have become attuned to. The scent of the magnolias lingers.

Aunty Esther and her tribe leave first on the Saturday morning.

'Goodbye, my darling,' she cries, hugging me tight. 'Kura! Tevita! Ngatokorua! Noʻoputa! Tua! Come give your cousin a kiss.'

They don't. They drag their bags and blankets out of the house and stuff them into empty spaces in their van.

Uncle Tiare says goodbye next. 'When my next lot of avocados come out, my niece, I'll send you a few and you can plant your own tree if you want.'

Aunty Esther overhears him. 'Eh, what foolishness are you filling her head with?' she cries. 'An avocado tree . . . *in Porirua*!'

She ushers the last of her tribe out the front door; Uncle Tiare trails behind them.

Aunty Teina leaves next. 'Auē,' she cries, and I sink into her arms. Now when she teases me with her usual questions, the awkwardness is gone. 'Better let your Aunty know when you get a boyfriend,' she says in her serious voice. 'You're old enough now. Do we need to have the talk before I leave?'

When I assure her we don't, the disappointment on her face is more than I can take.

Aunty Selina leaves last. 'My goddaughter,' she says, holding me for a second embrace. 'Don't forget, you can call me anytime, OK, honey?' She presses into my hand a business card with Uncle Craig's name on it. The phone number is circled in red and beside it are the words *call collect*, scribbled in my aunty's handwriting.

When she pulls me in for another hug, I feel her gold crucifix against my chest. It doesn't burn into my skin like I would've imagined once. I promise her I'll call, without moving my lips.

Uncle Craig follows her out the door with their first-class baggage.

I worry the house will feel empty once the aunties have gone. The sitting room looks like its old self again – the chairs and couch are back in their usual places; the cabinet is cleared of part-melted candlesticks. The rooms are empty of guests. There are no dead pigs hanging from the clothesline. No uncles in the garage with flagons of beer. No cousins crimping hair into tumbleweed in the bedroom. No aunties in the kitchen yelling orders at the cousins. No decades of the Rosary. No over-earnest singing. No mainese. No magnolias. No casket. No Mum.

Just home.

Love Rules for Island Girls

If he's an island boy, make sure he's not related. Second cousins is legal, I think, but first cousins is OK too – as long as you don't get pregnant. Find out where his family's from and find out who his mama is. Is she a kind island mama? Is she a mean island mama? Is she both kinds of island mama depending on which way you're looking? This will tell you what kind of boy you got. First and foremost, pay attention to these details.

Never talk to your folks about boys or sex. Your father will sulk and wonder how he raised a harlot. He'll blame it on your mother's side – he knew your aunties were trouble from day one – and your mother will think you're pregnant. She'll start planning your wedding. She'll pray the father's a white boy, or a doctor or the son of a minister if he's an island boy instead. Then they'll simmer in self-pity after making you feel bad too.

So please don't break your parents' hearts like that, and save yourself the grief.

Talk to your cousins about sex and boys. You know the kind of cousins – of the female persuasion. When you sneak out to meet your island boy, take one of these cousins with you. See if he flinches when he sees her beside you. Watch how he treats her when he serves up the leftovers. When you're sitting on his couch eating chicken and watching Netflix, see if he tries to sidle up next to you.

If the side of his thigh rests against yours and you hear his breath as he inhales and exhales and you see his chest, out of the corner of your eye – don't be obvious; don't make eye contact yet – rise and fall, the musky scent from his supermarket aftershave turning your head like a spin cycle, that means he's got past her. He's pleased the gatekeeper. She's given him the green light. Be cool. You got this. Let him lead you to another room.

Your cousin won't mind waiting.

After a while – like weeks, not hours – sit down with him and have the 'ex' talk.

Some things to ask: How many? Then how often, when, where, and was it any good? Where did you meet? Why'd you break up? Did her mother like you? Does her mother *know* you? Would you take her back? Did you cheat on her? Did she cheat on you? If we broke up and she took you back, would you cheat on her again? If we broke up and you took her back and she cheated on you, would you take her back *again*?

Was she a white girl?

And then let bygones be bygones. Life's too short to stress over exes. Just be grateful his standards are higher now.

Make sure he has a regular job, and look out for clues he still lives with his folks. You know the signs: velvet paintings of Jesus, school certificates beside the family photos, nativity scenes, plastic flowers, woven mats and baskets, rosary beads, shell necklaces, the Bible, crucifixes, tīvaevae covers on the cushions, the plastic sheet on the couch.

But if he's at university, cut the boy some slack – especially if he's studying medicine or law or business. If he's studying the arts, throw him to the fishes. If you don't do it, you know your mama will. But don't be mean about it. He's a sensitive soul – an aspiring poet, maybe – so proceed with caution. If you're not careful, he'll hit the big time and generations of students will learn to despise you. He might not have a regular job now, but make sure it's part of the long-term plan.

If he's a white boy, he might not get the deal with your cousin. Put the boy at ease. Tell him she's good and you needed her to drive you there – that's all. Watch his reaction. See if he flinches. Don't make him feel guilty but imply that he's racist if he dares to object.

Your cousin can sit at the same table if she wants. If she does, see how he treats her when she orders her meal. Order a large mochaccino with marshmallows on the side. Choose the dish with the heftiest price tag and eat it with relish. Eat it like you're paying for it. No – eat it like it's free. Because it *should* be free. Neither you nor your cousin will be forking up a cent. When he offers to pay for your food, always take it with grace. If you order the chicken, remember to eat it in this order: thigh, drumstick, wings, breast, back.

Be wary if he lets you eat the back of the chicken, though. He may as well be feeding you bones. Skinny bones that snap too easily between your tongue and the roof of your mouth. Skinny bones that get stuck in your throat. Skinny bones like the white girls he dated before you.

Don't be one of those girls who won't eat. Nobody likes fake girls like that. Plus, you're an island girl – he'll see right through it. And you'll just go home hungry and have to cook your own eggs.

Watch how the cousin acts at the table. If her voice becomes quiet so that all you can hear is the boy's bad jokes or the nervous tap of his fingers on the tabletop, it means he's played his cards right and the cousin approves. She'll play with her cellphone and say she has to leave early. Let her go. You got this, girl. Grab your coat and follow him to his car.

If he's a white boy, your mama will have a say in it. Be prepared.

Plaza de Toros

The noise from the arena can be heard outside, from the stand selling bamboo fans made in Taiwan. Queues of people line up to get in. Many of them are dressed in quick-drying travelling shorts with mix-and-match T-shirts made from hemp and organic cotton. Jandals or flip-flops or thongs slap against the sun-heated cobblestones. Heavy cameras, underused and overpaid for, are worn like lanyards round their necks. They dab at their sweaty cheeks and foreheads with cotton handkerchiefs, the sunscreen and insect repellent applied earlier in the day soiling the fabric. Many of them speak in heavy accents – sometimes in English, sometimes in Spanish. Sometimes in a language you don't quite recognise.

This is your third bullfight. This is how you spend your Saturday afternoons now.

You climb the internal concrete stairs and wait for the first round to end. The doors to the arena will eventually reopen. When they do, you go in. Your naked face smacks the shield of heat once more. You gasp and drown in the humidity, taking little wasp breaths as you weave your way up to one of the middle rows.

The wives and girlfriends of the bullfighters are in front of you, but you never worry about getting caught. They never look back. You noticed this about them the first time you watched them. So you sit two rows exactly behind *her*, so that when he's in the arena teasing the crowd, gesticulating with choreographed hand and head movements, and he turns her way and blows a kiss in the air, you can catch it. You watch it sweep across the circular dirt pit and float above the heads of the other onlookers like a decapitated dandelion. You snatch it and you guard it and, later, you pull it out from the shadows of your memory and place it beneath your pillow.

You lay your head upon it and dream.

Fanfare fills the stadium. The peal of trumpets alerts the crowd and a chariot with three horses trots around the edge of the bullring. The animals, resplendent in red and yellow flags and gold and silver adornments, are escorted into the arena by men in blue trousers with stripes of scarlet flames running down their sides. Their shirts are unblemished, taut and crisp, and their blue hats remind you of the caps your father wore to the greyhound races in Addington. The men are poised and alert like a row of soldiers, and the horses, joined by chains, strut between them, in a trance. The leader carries a whip. It's brown, not black and frayed like the one you kept hidden under your bed back home, which makes you smile. You try not to think about it – what he could use his whip for.

You live in cotton dresses and singlets and shorts that cling to your skin as soon as you leave your hostel. The sun is hot, but it doesn't burn like you're used to, and although your face, your neck, your arms, your legs are darker, browner, and that makes you self-conscious amongst these European crowds, your skin doesn't peel. It doesn't dry up and flake away from your cheekbones. Instead, your skin glows like lit barbecue charcoal as the horses are led out of the ring.

*

Your father was a man's man. He loved racing and rugby and protecting his girl. So when he found out you finally dumped Manu, it pleased him.

'I'm sorry, baby.'

'No you're not, Dad.' The silence confirmed it.

'Look,' he said, 'you're better off without him. That island boy was holding you back.'

'We're islanders too! And you always say that. They're never good enough for you – brown, black or . . . *blue.*'

'No, they're never good enough for *you.*'

It was Manu's idea to catch a bullfight.

'It's not like watching a rugby game, you know,' you argued. 'The animals actually die.'

Las Ventas was a popular bullring near the budget hotel you'd booked for a treat. After six months of backpacking through Europe, you'd slept in plenty of hostel rooms shared with other travellers. Many of them Australian. Like Jack – Jack the Australian.

'Running of the bulls. Heard of it, mate?' Both you and Manu had shrugged. 'It's the scariest thing I've ever done,' said Jack. 'Scarier than that time I killed a snake with my bare hands.'

'That tree snake?' you asked.

'It was dark, and I didn't know it was a tree snake.'

Manu was always up for a new adventure. That's what you loved about him in the beginning. The way he showed up at your flat on a Saturday, the borrowed tent and sleeping bags in the boot. The Post-it notes inside your university library books. The bad poetry. The drunken karaoke. The day you met his mama.

'You are from Christchurch?'

'Yes, Mama.'

'And your father? Where is he from?'

'Rarotonga,' you said. 'He came over to study and play rugby. But he got an injury at work and couldn't play rugby anymore.'

'And your mother? Where is she?'

'Divorced. Dad brought me up. It's just me and him.'

Mama frowned and then raised a bowl to your face. 'Chop suey?'

You don't know why it surprised you that Manu hadn't told her you were vegetarian. You left the pork belly pieces from the chop suey on your plate, and later you heard them being scraped from the plate into the rubbish bag. This, you tell yourself, is why his mama hated you.

Still, Manu had chutzpah. At least in the beginning.

'Come on, babes,' he'd said. 'It's not like we have to run with them. We'll be safe in the stands. They can't get us from there. They won't even *see* us. They probably wear blinkers.'

That last bit horrified you. No, you told him. *Fuck* no.

But as you both lay in your private budget-hotel bed, his fingers crawling over your bare thighs, his breath on your face, his tongue sliding down the side of your neck, you relented. And hand in hand you walked to Las Ventas, your jandals slapping the burning concrete. You joined the throng of tourists, whose sunburnt cheeks and fanny packs gave them away. You climbed those concrete steps to your seats in the Heavens and you peered through plastic binoculars you wished you'd left behind.

And that's when you first saw him. José. The matador.

The only thing that protected him from the charging bull was his cape, a flimsy piece of fabric versus a human-killing animal. He didn't even have a horse he could ride away on like the picadors. It shocked you that it excited you to be this close to death. To know that this man, this mere mortal man, could die in front of you. You didn't think twice about your attraction to him, and the thought of stripping off his bravado and having his vulnerability exposed to you, just you, even for that one night, excited you even more.

'He's a what?' your dad would ask.

'A matador, Dad.'

'A matador?'

'Yes, Dad. He's an athlete. A professional athlete. Like an All Black but more dangerous.'

'He kills innocent animals for a living?'

'Dad?'

'Yes, daughter?'

'You worked at the freezing works, or did you forget?'

That evening after the bullfights, while you and Manu sat in the bar across the road from your cheap hotel – him sinking a jug of beer, you a jug of sangria – you spotted him, José, sitting on one of the stools. The rage inside your gut, which churned like hot chilli when you spotted the young groupies with him, caught you off guard. You couldn't hear him from your table, but you could see him, and he was as animated in that bar as he was in the bullring. He laughed openly, unselfconsciously, from the belly in a way that reminded you of home. Your aunties and uncles and cousins. Your dad. You craved a piece of that homeliness.

Manu went to the bar for another round of drinks. You tried to be discreet, but José had noticed you noticing him, and by the time he crossed the room to say a friendly 'hola', you'd already decided what you wanted to do. The next day, you turned up at the hotel room you shared with Manu, packed your backpack, and moved into the hostel.

The crowd in the stadium roars, filling your head like expanding foam. The sight of the bullfighters still amuses you. Manly. Masculine. Macho. *Pink* – pink and yellow capes, pink socks with flats, flats with gold buckles.

It sickens you to watch these fights, but it thrills you to see your man on the battlefield. It thrills you to watch the crowd work themselves up. You think of Roman gladiators and Russell Crowe.

They release the bull. You know by now that the first few victims are the runts. At that first bullfight, you were shocked by the size of the first bull you saw and you fretted over the safety of the picador, who circled the bullring on horseback, armed only with a single lance. But after being prodded and teased for many agonising minutes, the bull's charges becoming less frantic and its reactions more relenting, it was finally put out of its misery, and by the time the next bull had entered the pit, your allegiance had shifted.

The bull stamps across the ring, urged on by the picador. It's poked and it's aggravated and when it charges at the bullfighter, you're pleased that it does. You hope that the bullfighter will fall off his horse, trip over his flats, rip the frills on his blouse. When he jumps behind one of the safety barriers, you simmer at the unfairness. You want to run down to the ring and shove him back in, tell him to pick on someone his own size, like an average-sized woman.

'Olé!' screams the crowd.

You peer down at the *other halves*, owning the stadium like footballers' wives. From the back they seem uninterested, with their sweatless, taut bodies and unfrizzable hairdos. You look over at *her*. You've seen her face only twice. Once in a photograph on his bedside table and then last week while you waited in line to get in. She sashayed past as if you were part of the souvenir stand.

The picador prods the bull with his pica, eventually thrusting it with enough force to pierce the back of the bull's neck. A second pica is stabbed into its back. They waggle like your acupuncture needles. Again the bull charges, but slower this time, as the picador jumps another barrier.

One of the matadors runs into the ring, flapping his cape to distract the bull. You watch in horror as the bull rushes for it, knowing the bullfighter will step aside. When he throws the cape, it gets caught in the bull's horns, blocking the bull's sight as it loses its bearings.

'Olé!'

The bull slows down. When the matador stabs his sword between its shoulder blades, the bull digs its hooves into the dirt. It pushes its haunches out and suspends its front legs in the air. You're close enough to hear its cries. The noise punches you in the throat and your body lurches.

The bullfighter spurs on the crowd like a rock star, circling the ring and striking the air with his fist. The crowd takes the bait. The energy in the arena is heightened by their cheering, their desperation to witness more death. The bull, barely conscious, struggles to stand as the matador prances around its disabled form. With one final heave, the bull collapses. It lies in the pit and dies.

'Olé!'

The first three rounds of fights are grisly enough, but you know they will only get worse from here, and you've witnessed the slaughtering of two bulls already. *You've witnessed the slaughtering of two bulls.*

You know José is next and the thought of him in his finery excites you. The way he glitters reminds you of the mirror ball in the bar the night you met. When Manu came back with the drinks, José was showing you a scar on his forearm from the time he nearly got killed.

'Hola,' he said when he saw Manu hovering. 'José.' He offered his hand and Manu took it. In the fragmented light from the mirror ball, you caught glimpses of the whites in their knuckles. Their eyes were locked and you were encouraged by this. You could tell by the way José had reached out to you that affections like this were normal. This is what you remembered when you fought with Manu when he wanted to leave. You remembered this when you went home with José.

José struts to the centre of the bullring. The crowd's reaction pleases you. As expected, he turns your way.

He raises his hand to his lips, then waves his open palm at you, inducing another cheer from the crowd, which makes you blush and hold your breath as you watch his invisible kiss float high above the heads of the men, the women, the wives, the girlfriends – *her*. You reach out to catch it and through splayed fingers you watch as he stares at you, his kiss now trapped between your fingertips, and at that instant you see *her* put her hand to her face and wave at him, so you do the same, kissing the fingertips of your free hand, blowing gently, letting your breath carry your kiss to him, high above the heads of the men and the women and the wives and the girlfriends and *her*, and you watch him pluck it from the air, lock it in his fist and stamp his chest with it, so you do the same, pressing your fist with his locked-up kiss against your breast.

The crowd roars one final time as a bull enters the pit. José eyeballs the animal. His back is stiff. His feet are set wide apart. You watch him fan out his cape, attracting the bull's attention. The bull is bigger than the others you've seen that day and you panic even though you know to expect this. You know not to worry about him, but you do. You worry about him as if he were as fragile as that defenceless animal.

The bull kicks one of its hind legs into the dirt, winding itself up like a toy. Dirt particles rise from the ground. José waves his cape, half of the fabric now concealing him from the bull's stony gaze. He waves the cape to the other side and this time the bull charges.

'Olé!'

The bull thunders towards José, ignoring the cape and the crowd and the cheering. But the horror of man and animal colliding, the sight of José losing his footing, the hard landing on his back, the rubber limbs, the snap of his neck are second to what comes next.

You watch her jump to her feet. You watch her race down the steps towards the bullring. You watch as the bull is hustled out of the ring and you watch her run into the centre of the pit. She drops to her knees. She cradles his head in her lap. And for the first time since you started coming to these bullfights, you scream.

Love Rules from Island Mama

For Island Girls

If you want the good husband to marry, make sure he not the bad man. To know he not the bad man, see that he good to his mama. This the most important thing. The good son is the good husband to marry. Here the things how you know it true.

One, he visit his mama in the week. At least the one time, but more is better. He should go to the house where he was a boy in the old days. He should drive to the church on the Sunday with his mama. Even though he don't believe in the God stuff no more, if he sit by his mama where all the other mamas can see, then God will forgive him because he the good son. He is better than their son. Their son is the bad man. Their son don't drive their mama to the church because they don't believe in the God stuff no more. They spend the payday on the Lotto and the horse and the beer, and on the Sunday they have no money for the church collection. Make sure he not the bad son like them. The bad son like the bad man.

Two, if he not live near his mama anymore, then he should talk to his mama on the telephone. At least the two time in the week, but more is better. And always, always on the birthday and the Mother Day. And early in the day, before it time to go to church. So the mama can tell all the other mamas what a good son is he. And always he should pay the call for himself. Not call in the collect way and his mama have to pay. And flowers. On the birthday and the Mother Day always. If he can't drive the mama to the church on the Sunday, this the least he can do.

Three, he should pay for the Sky TV and the internet machine for the computer box. He should pay for the power bill so the mama can use them. Even though she will not. But still. If he pay all these things but not for the power bill and the power in the house is gone, no more, that make him the cheap man. And the stupid man. Don't marry the stupid man. He worse than the bad man.

Four, make sure he know how to make the babies. But don't make the babies before the wedding time. When you know he know how to do the thing, make sure it with you and only you. Make sure he want to do the thing to make the babies too. After the wedding time, only after the wedding time.

If he bring you to his mama home, it mean he told her about you already. It mean he not scared what his mama think. It mean he like you. It mean he might love you. Watch how he treat his mama. That how you know he the good man or not.

For Island Boys

If you want the good wife to marry, make sure she not the cheeky girl. To know she not the cheeky girl, see how she treat your mama. This the most important thing. When she come to your mama house and she eat like the picky picky bird, she the cheeky girl. If she leave the chicken bones on the plate with the chicken meat still on the bones, she the cheeky girl. If she wipe the coconut cream off the coconut bun because she say it make her the fat girl, she the cheeky girl. And probably she too skinny. Don't trust the skinny girl. She the cheeky girl too.

Make sure she come from the good family. Make sure she got the good family values. Make sure she know the island family ways. Because if she want to be the good wife to marry, she got to know her place. To know she come from the good family, see how she treat *her* mama. This the second most important thing. The third most important: she can cook the island food.

Don't go with the girl who don't know how to cook the island food. Her food won't be as good as your mama food. This, I swear on the Holy Bible. But she should know how to bake the taro leaves. She should know how to make the chop suey. She should know how to fry the Rarotongan doughnuts. Even if she too skinny to eat the island food. If she don't know how to cook the island food, then how she will look after your babies?

Make sure she know how to make the babies. But don't make the babies before the wedding time. If she try to, she might be the cheeky girl underneath. If this happen, look at her mama. Her mama might be the cheeky girl in the old day. That how you know what you gonna end up with.

When you know she know how to do the thing, make sure it with you and only you. Make sure she want to do the thing to make the babies too. But only after the wedding time, don't forget.

Don't marry the lazy girl. The lazy girl bad like the cheeky girl. If she come to your mama house and the kettle sing in the kitchen like the mamas in the 'ūtē and she sit on the couch and wait, she the lazy girl. She probably the stupid girl too. Don't marry the stupid girl. She worse than the cheeky girl.

If she bring you to her mama home, it mean she told her about you already. It mean she not scared what her mama think. It mean she like you. It mean she might love you. Watch how she treat her mama. That how you know she the good wife to marry.

But watch out for her papa.

Beats of the Paʻu

Sunday, 4 July 1976
On the first Sunday of each month, Father O'Shea leads Raro Mass, his Irish accent pulling the language into awkward shapes and sounds. The youngest children, who sit on the front pew, giggle behind cupped hands, their ears not yet tuned to this twisted version of their parents' mother tongue. Even if they were used to the way the words tumble from his mouth, the way the words hang suspended in the room like floating helium balloons, they still wouldn't know their meaning. As they do during the English Masses every other Sunday of the month, the children mimic the actions of the older ones behind them. Stand. Sit. Kneel. Pray.

They pray.

Terepai, one of the aunties, prays for her only daughter. She prays that bastard boyfriend of her daughter's will disappear. She prays for forgiveness for swearing in church. She prays for guidance.

Her daughter, Katerina, runs her hand gently over her belly. It's concealed beneath her baggy maxi dress, the fabric billowing over her tiny bump. She prays for her boyfriend, that he will love her forever – forever and ever and ever. Amen.

Stand, sit, kneel, pray. And every now and then they sing, the words of the hymns delivered in that other language, words the children on the front pew have learned to mimic like a nursery rhyme, their tongues curled round the letters, their voices projecting the syllables with ease.

Terepai's voice meets the wooden slats of the lofty ceiling. Her virtuous notes are decibels above the rest. She crows like a rooster at the break of dawn, beckoning the angels, so there's no doubt in anyone's mind that the good Lord is listening. How could He not, with a voice like hers? Even Father O'Shea is caught off guard, his Cook Islands Māori now more stilted and whinnying.

Later, Terepai's older brother Rahui rises to his feet. He flattens his suit jacket, tugging at its hem, pushing out his chin, his eyeline raised. He saunters over to the pulpit, his sermon – scribbled bullet-points on three pages torn from his daughter's school book – folded discreetly inside his hand.

Father O'Shea, his eye forever on the future of his parish, makes sure to involve the community leaders. So the people can see their own during proceedings. It's his way of guaranteeing his followers remain in line, generation after generation – by handpicking the catechists himself, young couples with growing broods. Stable and reliable and not afraid to speak up.

Katerina waits until her uncle is settled behind the wooden podium before averting her eyes. The confessional booths to her right look enticing. She wishes she could enter one of them and disappear. She's willing to commit sins for the privilege.

After the church service, Katerina congregates with the relatives outside. It's her favourite part of Raro Mass, the gathering after, like a post-match debrief of the week's shenanigans. No more than a week goes by without them catching up on each other's business. Theirs is a close-knit community, growing by the minute, built from scratch by the generations before. Pioneering aunts and uncles, grandparents, sacrificing havens in the tropics for harsher climates and the daily grind. Katerina is grateful for her village of nurturing elders. She belongs somewhere, is part of something. But every now and then, in times of self-reflection, she dares to imagine freedom and finds the affiliation suffocating.

As usual, the relatives flock within their designated zones. The youngest cousins levitate around the knees of their mothers. Katerina and the older cousins detach from the pack, perching like magpies on the concrete barrier by the road. There they preen themselves, prodding 'fros with Afro combs and checking lips glossed with Vaseline. They gabble excitably, safely out of earshot from prying parents and open to being leered at by strangers in cars.

This is where Katerina feels her safest – with her cousins, and with her best friend and cousin Luana by her side. She feels a nudge in her ribs and awaits the spectacle, watching Luana pull at the fold of her off-white skivvy. The unsightly bruise at the base of her neck is exposed. The shenanigans begin.

'Last night,' announces Luana, the blood rushing through her cheeks. 'At the dance.'

Katerina recalls the grass clippings in her hair. The cousins crowd round, admiring the hickey. They shuffle impatiently on the spot, fearful of missing out on the gossip. Katerina is optimistic that they will not. Luana delights in the show and tell of idle talk, so by the time their parents are ready to leave, the salacious facts have been safely passed on.

Promises of silence are made between the cousins, the girls crossing their hearts and hoping to die, swearing on a loved one's grave for good measure.

Saying goodbye is a protracted affair. When it's time to leave, the execution is military, like they're platoons divided by household locality. In the beginning, they climb the small hill past the church as one, stopping at the entrance of Bedford Street and then the intersection at Champion Street by the petrol station. Slowly their numbers drop as each family advances towards their own home. The cousins split up, Luana bidding the most dramatic farewell, and by the time they turn into Warspite Avenue and are walking past the Cannons Creek shops – the TAB, the fruit shop, the New World supermarket – it's just Katerina and two younger cousins left. She lights up a smoke and sucks on the filtered tip, trapping the fumes in her lungs before letting them out in a single breath.

'Want one, cuz?' she asks, half joking. The box is open in front of them, its flip-top pulled back to expose the smoke butts.

Moana, the older of the two, stares down into the box. Each smoke fits snugly like a piece in a puzzle, and Katerina is surprised that it makes her feel sentimental. All of a sudden, it feels wrong to break up the symmetry, its appearance of belonging. She's convinced her young cousin will rightly refuse, and when she doesn't, she regrets asking.

'Help yourself, cuz.' She sounds more enthusiastic than she feels. She will have to feed her Doublemint gum long before the girls reach home.

Moana slides a smoke out from the pack, creating a dent in one of the rows. It forces the other smokes to crowd at clumsy angles, like shifting teeth compensating for years of missing premolars. Katerina holds the lighter between them. The tiny flame flickers from the tip of her thumb. She thinks of Mahuika, the Māori goddess of fire, and she convinces herself that this is how a goddess is. With the earth at her feet and the promise of fire forever at her fingertips.

Moana's smoke kisses the dancing flame and she takes little moth breaths, the fumes burning in her throat for a second as she coughs. The amber glow at the tip of her smoke turns black from lack of encouragement. Moana looks betrayed.

'Let me, cuz.' Katerina takes the smoke, presses the tip against her own and inhales until it begins to smoulder. She tries to make eye contact with Moana but she is avoiding her, and Katerina can feel the shame of her young cousin's failure. She reassures her with no derision or judgement, just guiding words. 'Breathe it in slowly, cuz,' she says, handing back the smoke. 'Hold it in your lungs and then breathe it out. It'll burn for a second but you'll get used to it with practice.' She demonstrates with her own cigarette, inhaling and holding her breath before the release.

Moana tries again. First she inhales, choking when the fumes hit the back of her throat. She pauses to make time for the burning in her mouth and the coughing to die down. The second time the burning is less severe, the coughing less persistent.

'See?' says Katerina. 'I told you it gets easier, cuz.'

By the time Moana's tried a fifth time, Katerina can see she knows to expect the burn. She's learned to control her throat muscles in anticipation. She knows to hold her breath, to pause and let the sensation run through her. Inhale. Hold. Exhale. This makes Katerina smile.

'You girls got a boyfriend?' she asks.

The colour rushes up Moana's face. 'Boys round here too ugly.'

Katerina is relieved. Smoking is one thing. 'I got a boyfriend,' she tells them. 'A man, actually. A lover.' It feels good to release her secret, to tell somebody she trusts, somebody with no vested interest. She feels lighter, cleansed, forgiven – as if she needed to be forgiven. She will tell Luana, in time.

Moana is concentrating hard on the smoke. She stills her breath, trapping the fumes. Inhale. Hold. And then exhale.

'We're getting married. But don't tell my mum.'

Katerina's younger cousins shake their heads, speechless and flattered. The fumes get caught in Moana's throat and her throat muscles start to spasm. She begins to cough.

'She'll beat me with the island broom,' says Katerina, 'then tell me I can't have a boyfriend till I'm married.' She laughs nervously, smacking Moana's back until her coughing subsides.

'Promise, cuz,' Moana says once she's finally composed.

When they reach their street, Katerina gives each of the girls a stick of gum, smelling Moana's breath just before their house is visible. She watches them walk up their driveway and waits until they're inside, waving at Uncle Rahui, who's waiting for his daughters at the front door, before walking past four more houses and turning into her driveway. Her next-door neighbour Fetu is sitting outside his house in his taxi in his Sunday best. He raises his head at her. She ignores him.

Katerina lets herself in the back door, placing the spare key back under the rock beside her mother's Daphne plant. Its perfume is stronger than usual and she tries to bury the scent in her gut. When she enters the kitchen, the chicken is still roasting in the oven, the fat spitting against the inside of the oven door. The aroma, mingled with the scent of the Daphne, makes her dry retch, her stomach churning. She flees the kitchen and shuts herself in her bedroom where she can take a few deep breaths. Her stomach begins to settle. She slowly undresses in front of the mirror, checking her reflection, examining herself from every angle.

The bump is barely visible, but to her it stands out like Te Manga. She's not seen the magnificent mountain in person, but has heard about it from her mother, who used to climb to its summit as a young girl. She knows enough about it now to know its beauty and strength, and whenever she manifests it in her mind's eye, she feels its presence like it is a living part of her. The ferns and plants alive with the local fauna, the trees tall and majestic, towering over Rarotonga like leafy bodyguards.

She slides her fingers over her swollen belly. Her baby is still small enough to cradle in the palm of her hand, like a wooden clothes peg. When she was at primary school, she'd made a family of wooden clothes pegs, which she kept hidden in a shoebox tucked under her bed. Mama Peg, Papa Peg and identical twin girls – identical to make it fair, and twins so they'd never be alone. She named them and gave them imaginary lives, clothing them in strips of leftover fabric her mother kept in a pillowcase beside her sewing machine.

Her baby is the size of a wooden clothes peg.

She runs her hands down her front, imagining they're the hands of her lover. She closes her eyes and remembers his promise. His scent. His touch. The music that was playing. It's playing in her head now, on loop, last night's slow waltz soldered into her memory.

'Katerina! Katerina? Where you?'

Katerina plods down the corridor towards the sitting room, where her mother has planted herself on the couch. Her feet press into the fraying carpet, the rough ridges rubbing against her soles. The friction makes her fully aware, needlessly self-conscious of every inch of herself. This is only made worse when she hears a second voice in the room.

'That's why, Mrs Torea, I don't like the Kiwi girls. They dress like hookers and they have no self-respect,' Eugene says, naturally shifting to broken English. 'Even the island girls who think they the Kiwi girls, they too much try to do like the Papa'a way.'

Katerina acknowledges Eugene before taking a seat in the chair opposite her mother. She notices how deflated he is and hopes the girls from last night are choking on their lunch.

'You know what, Mrs Torea?' he says. 'When I'm older I will go to the islands and find myself a beautiful vaine. We will live on the beach in a hut made from pandanus leaves and rocks collected from the foot of the mountain. We'll eat coconuts and mangoes that grow wild around us, and catch plenty seafood. The land and ocean will be our supermarket. Our tamariki will run carefree – no shoes, just shorts – that's all they need. And in the night time we will dance in the moonlight to the quick, steady beats of the pa'u.'

Katerina watches for her mother's reaction. She looks much older than her thirty-three years. Not in her face – which is still unlined, though her cheekbones have become more prominent as the years have progressed – but in her pensive stares, in the way her shoulders slump and her homemade frock hangs off her delicate frame. In the way she barely notices her daughter.

Katerina breaks the silence. 'Mum?'

Her mother flinches, snapping out of her trance. 'Where have you been? Who have you been with?'

'Nowhere, Mum. I came straight home.'

'With who?'

'The girls.'

'What girls?'

Katerina fails to stop herself from sighing.

'What girls?'

'Moana and Tere.'

'Who else?'

'No one else.'

'You sure?'

Katerina turns away from her mother's tired face. She inspects the carpet for food crumbs and finds none. Her mother has swept away the mess already, in the way she always does.

'Why are you late? It shouldn't take you this long. Are you sure you didn't go anywhere? See anyone else?'

Katerina locks her gaze on her mother's, but there's a knowing in her mother's eyes that makes her look away.

'Nowhere else, Mum. I came straight home.'

Eugene is silent. He stares at the TV screen as if he's searching for his vaine. A conga line of people is snaking its way through the television studio, celebrating Telethon's latest donation update. Katerina is relieved to see him there. His presence – always unbidden, never unwelcomed – softens the tension between her and her mother.

Katerina excuses herself and leaves the room to check on the chicken. In the kitchen she opens the back door to let out the bad air and suddenly craves another smoke. The image of Moana trying her first cigarette makes her cringe and smile. But she can't have one now. Her mother is more jumpy than usual, and she doesn't want a repeat of the other day.

'You want to burn the house down with that?'

Katerina and Luana wagged class on Tuesday. They spent the afternoon dragging on menthol smokes behind the house. Before Katerina could blink, Luana answered for them, greeting the livid Terepai with a kiss on the cheek, the smoke strong on her breath. The welts from the vacuum cleaner hose are still healing.

Katerina sets the table for three and they sit in silence. She picks apart her drumstick with her fingers, alternating between peeling the skin from the flesh and the flesh from the bone. Plays with her wristwatch, watching the seconds-hand inch its way around the clock face. Tomorrow, things will be different.

Saturday, 3 July

When my daughter was born, the nurses in the maternity ward would fuss over her. She's so beautiful, they would say. She's going to break hearts someday. They said it like it wasn't a curse, as if it were something I should hang on my wall. Imagine that, bragging about your daughter's good looks like they are a woven basket or a garland of plastic hibiscus. Katerina had always been a pretty girl, and because of that I feared for her and the years that lay ahead. It wasn't pride I felt. People I'd never met before would stop me in the street, desperate to get a closer look at her, like an exhibition or something that belonged to them also. Even the pram the nuns loaned me, with its plastic rain cover that concealed all but the top of her head, couldn't discourage prying eyes. She was a tall baby, a long baby, and back then, before she could even walk, I could see she was quick. Desperate to run away. To break free from things she thought were holding her back. When my daughter was born, I was barely a baby myself. Not only young, but helpless. Frightened. Alone.

'Iron those clothes before you come out tonight. The dance starts at six. Don't be late for it.'

I watched my daughter trying not to moan. It had become a regular thing now, her holding herself back from reacting, monitoring her actions. Her movements were becoming stiff and crude like an old woman's. And she was getting fat. It frustrated me to watch her age so prematurely, and at the same time act so childlike.

'What's the matter? You got somewhere more important to be?' I was beginning to despise that wristwatch. It seemed to occupy her more and more these days.

'No.'

'And clean the bathroom. Do it properly. You didn't do it properly last week.' I gave her fuller instructions: 'Wipe the taps with a clean cloth. Make sure there are no streaks. Scrub the bath. Mop the floor. Put on some potatoes.' Then I watched her drag her feet around the house, silent and full of resentment. She tidied up the bedrooms with equal contempt. But at least she was safe and keeping out of trouble, as long as I could see her.

Her eyes reminded me of her father's. Her spiked eyelashes, standing forever erect from the base of her eyelids, looked to me like the stems of the island broom. When she was younger, I would tease her about them, and my brother would scold me in private, tell me it wasn't her fault that he left.

I wasn't that much older than she is now when she was born. And the older she gets the more I see myself in her too. She never knew her father. He'd disappeared as soon as he found out I was carrying, long before I was nursing her in that maternity ward, sharing the joy of first-time motherhood with strangers. Before then, he said we would marry. Build a home of our own and fill it with children.

Just before I left the house, Katerina was starting on a load of washing. We don't own a machine so I had to make sure she piled the dirty sheets and pillowcases into the tub in the wash house. The water was steaming hot and soapy, the suds made from melting soap flakes, grated fresh. Never mind that the skin on her fingertips would shrivel up like boiled taro leaves, or that the heat from the water might burn her hands. Better she learned from me: life isn't a fairy tale.

*

Finally, Katerina had the house to herself. The weight of her mother's unhappiness made her tense. She relished the small window of freedom she was given, imagined it was real and longer-lasting. She felt trivial, burdensome, irrelevant around her mother, and it scared her to think they shared the same genes. She called her boyfriend, just to hear his voice.

'I will come over.'

'Don't be stupid.'

'Don't you miss me?'

'Not much.'

It felt good to laugh again.

'How long is the slave driver out?'

'She didn't say.'

'I will speak to her. If you let me.'

'No . . .' The thought of her mother and her boyfriend together felt too catastrophic. She could feel her heart pounding and knew instinctively that a sudden rise in blood pressure wouldn't be good for the baby. A smoke would've helped, but she couldn't risk getting caught again. She inhaled. Held her breath for a second. Exhaled. If things played out how she knew they should, the meeting was inevitable. But she didn't have to worry about that today.

After she hung up, she went back to the wash house, where the sheets and pillowcases were still soaking in the tub. The colour of her hands had returned to normal, not blistering pink, and the water was cooling. Her naked feet were cool against the unrelenting lino, and this seemed to stabilise her thoughts.

She made a beeline for the potato sack on the floor. Before reaching in, she could tell they were low. They would need just a few for the two of them, anyway, three or four spuds, which she pulled from the bag, feeling dirt at the bottom of the sack. Normally, it wasn't worth worrying about, but buying new potatoes required talking to her mother.

'Leave it.'

Her boyfriend's voice startled her. She hadn't heard him let himself in and she didn't have time to reprimand him before he pinned her against the wall, his body cocooning her, and pressed himself in the small of her back.

'The slave driver,' said Katerina, panicked. 'She might come home.'

The musky stench of his dry sweat was overpowering, his breath against the nape of her neck leaving a cold spot. His hands were warm and damp and tender, sliding down her shoulders, cupping her elbows; their fingers interlocked for an instant before he reached around and squeezed her breasts. She flinched at his touch and he ignored it, moving his hand to her belly. He paused there, caressing her in circular strokes, gently kneading her flesh through the fabric. His fingers massaged her until she relented, her shoulders slackening, her body reclining. She leaned back into him, the strength in his torso carrying them both. Then she opened her eyes and saw the potato sack, the tub full of tepid water and dirty sheets and pillowcases.

'Stop it,' she said, squirming. 'My mum.' She could barely get the words out and the hoarseness in her voice only excited him more. He pulled at the hem of her dress, lifting it so that the cool air brushed against her thighs. He ran one hand over her leg and stuck his fingers inside the gusset of her underwear, flicking her gently. The silence in the wash house was broken only by the unbuckling of his belt and the metal teeth of his zipper as it was being pulled apart.

He grabbed her hand and brought it behind her, guiding it down his Y-fronts, letting her fingers rake his pubes. He pushed the palm of her hand onto himself and moaned in her ear when she held him, his penis firming in her grip. She lost her balance for a second and they both collapsed against the wall, her face pressed up against the cladding. He stepped back. When she turned round to face him, he'd already peeled off his jeans and dropped them to the floor.

*

By the time I arrived at the community hall, the tables and chairs were nearly set up, my cousins and their older sons moving the furniture like they were carrying bits of cardboard. No strain or struggle – just smooth like clockwork, the tables long enough to seat a dozen people.

An intimate number so that secrets can be shared easily, but large enough to stop them from getting out of hand.

It feels necessary to keep myself busy these days. Working in the hall gives me purpose, but it also takes my mind off my daughter. I know she is at that difficult age that daughters reach, on the verge of womanhood, that time in their life when they believe they know everything. But I worry for her, that she will take that confidence of hers and commit to something bigger than she can handle, something she may need to face alone.

These church socials have always been a highlight for me, always held a place in my heart. It's where I met Katerina's father, not long after I came to this country, where his dancing hooked me and his charm and promises reeled me in. The way he moved; the way other women watched him move. He chose me, and that made me feel special. Little did I know that his love was conditional.

Being part of this community gave me something to hold on to – it pulled me back up when I couldn't see how. And I can tell by the way some of our young ones embrace it that our community is in good hands, likely to survive after my generation has passed. Even my niece Luana will remain. Despite her need to break rules, to push boundaries in a way that frustrates the older ones, she will stay, continue the cycle, keep our traditions alive.

This is why watching my daughter mope about the house, dragging her feet on the carpet, heavy like bricks, is exasperating. She doesn't realise how good she has it, how easy life can be for someone like her. As soon as she is able to, I know she will abandon this place, me, leave us behind, believing there's something better out there.

When I was her age, I believed the same thing. I believed

her father was my saviour, that he would steal me away from here and together we'd build a new life. I didn't know that freedom came at a price.

*

Later that evening, on the way to the dance, Katerina and Luana were in the back seat of Fetu's taxi.

'Funny ending up with your call, eh?' Fetu called out, watching them through his rear-vision mirror. 'Must be my lucky night.' His gaze lingered over Katerina for too long. She watched his eyes scanning her dress, aware that the contours of her body were creating soft curves beneath the fabric. He raised his head and met her gaze and when she smiled at him – her glossed lips pouting, her eyes burrowing – he looked away, suddenly shy, hands firmly on the steering wheel.

Except for the stars, which flickered like faint light bubbles, the sky was jet black. The streets were desolate, but Katerina could sense the life behind the closed curtains. Families gathered round glowing television sets, watching live acts from around the country. She wasn't delusional; she knew that was fantasy, that the reality was likely more jarring and raw. But she bathed in it, let it wash over her like waves in the sea. They drove past the church – Luana mock crossing herself – and continued down Mungavin Avenue until they could hear the throbbing notes from the electric bass spilling out of the community hall.

'Fuck,' cried Luana, 'hate this island shit.' Katerina turned to her, saw her thick eyeliner, her rubied lips, her long wavy hair tumbling down the sides of her face. Her cousin was beautiful, like a Polynesian temptress. 'Why don't they play some real music?'

Fetu laughed. Katerina noticed his laugh lines through the mirror. 'What you mean?' he said. 'This the best music. Listen to that drum beat. That's the sound of home.'

'Nah, bro. Not *my* home,' Luana said. 'The sound of my home is platform shoes. You know, Donna Summer; Earth, Wind and Fire; KC and the Sunshine Band.'

Fetu chuckled and, still facing the road, said, 'And what's wrong with your friend back there? Cat got her tongue?' He parked the car outside the dairy opposite the hall. Other dancegoers, many of them relatives, their identities exposed by the island embellishments on their frocks and shirts, crossed the road intermittently, letting the music lure them. 'Tell me, Luana, what kind of music is the sound of *her* home?'

In that moment, Katerina despised him. Feeling challenged and trapped, she stared out her window. She could see Luana grinning and braced herself.

'I think it's a hymn,' Luana joked. '"Ave Maria"?' Katerina felt smothered, enduring their hysterics. She wished her seat would open up and let her fall through.

Fetu waved away Luana's cash when she tried to pay the fare. He turned in his seat again, homing in on Katerina. 'Have fun tonight, girls – but not too much.'

Luana answered for them, dragging Katerina out the door. 'Can't make any promises, bro.'

As they made their way towards the hall, Katerina imagined Fetu still watching her. Her feet felt clumsy, her head giddy, and to make matters worse, they were late.

*

I knew this would happen. Nine twenty-two. Sometimes I wonder if she defies me on purpose, because she knows it upsets me, makes me look bad. She doesn't realise it now, but one day she will, when she's older and has her own children to worry about. Walking in here without a care in the world, acting as if she owns the place, like her time is more important than anybody else's. I just hope she's learned enough from me now to know what influences are right for her. Of course, she won't realise it but she still has so much more to learn.

I count my blessings every day. My life hasn't been easy, but it could've been worse. My brother Rahui has always been the greatest support to us, protected me with his life when he found out I was pregnant. He isn't that much older than me, was making his way in this new world, away from the family we left behind. But he defended me when our father disowned me, swore to take care of us and love my daughter like she were his. He was the father figure she lacked, and she looks up to him. It fills me with hope to watch her with his children, protecting them like siblings, proving to me she's capable of compassion.

She is wearing another saggy dress. It hangs off her like a dish rag, although she still looks beautiful. I can see the attention she gets, even when she's not trying – not that she's ever had to. I don't think she even likes it, the way people notice her. She gets that from me, would rather blend into the background than encourage unwanted eyes. I will not complain about them, the unflattering dresses she chooses to wear now. I would rather she cover herself up than expose her body for all the world to see. Like her cousin.

My daughter's tardiness, on the other hand – that did not come from me. Nor did her tendency to disobey rules. I know I can be relied on to get things done; that is my strength – to make things happen, put things right. Even when it feels like the whole world disagrees.

*

People were milling around outside the hall – aunties and uncles smoking, laughing, gossiping in that language the young ones found indecipherable. Their words mingling in the air with their cigarette smoke. Katerina and Luana joined their cousins round the side of the hall, helping themselves to quick swigs of beer from stolen flagons. The din from the hall – the music from the live band, the throngs of people gathered inside – became intoxicating, and it wasn't long before Luana was leading Katerina inside.

As usual, the doors were manned by a couple of aunties, dressed to the nines in their homemade frocks. Their freshly made 'ei katu were fitted like halos, their voices making up in volume what they lacked in size.

'Kia orana, girls.' The aunties spoke in chorus, a sprightly sing-song. They inspected their nieces' outfits, running their eyes over the length of each of them. Pausing at various body parts: face, torso, legs, feet.

'Luana,' said one, 'aren't you cold in that little dress?'

Katerina could feel Luana beside her brimming with pride. It would take more than blunt criticism to break her spirit.

'Where is your jacket, my niece?' asked the other. 'You want to borrow my cardigan?' The aunty reached for the white cardigan draped over the back of her chair.

'No, thank you, Aunty. I'm fine.' Luana smiled sweetly at her, but Katerina knew she wasn't done. 'I must have hot blood or something, Aunty. Runs in the family, I think.'

Katerina heard the aunties mumbling under their breath as she followed Luana into the hall.

'Katerina.'

Before she even saw her, Katerina could picture her mother's tapping feet, her folded arms, the disappointment in her eyes. She turned, and the image in her head was standing before her.

'What took you so long to get here? I needed you to help out in the kitchen. I told you, you can't come unless you help out. You're not a little girl anymore. You have to do your bit.'

Katerina knew it was difficult for her mother to admit to herself that her daughter was growing up.

'I had to finish my jobs.'

'Did you iron the clothes?'

'Yes, Mum.' As soon as she said it she regretted it.

'Don't talk to me like that.'

Katerina sighed, which only exacerbated the situation. She could feel people watching them.

'Mum, I did everything you told me to do. Like always.'

'Except you here late.'

'I'm here now.'

Luana leaned in between them, discreetly pinching Katerina on the wrist. 'Hello, Aunty,' she crooned, kissing Terepai on the cheek.

'And *you*—' Katerina's mother shifted her attention to Luana. 'You better not make any trouble tonight.'

'No, Aunty,' said Luana. Her eyes grew wide. 'Of course not, Aunty. You know me.' She crossed her heart and kissed her fingers.

'Yes, my niece, I know you.' Terepai gave Katerina one final look before turning to go back into the kitchen.

Luana dragged Katerina into the hall. The lights were

dimmed but the dance floor was lit up with coloured bubbles that bounced off the mirror ball and onto the walls around them. The band was onstage, filling the room with 'Quando, Quando, Quando', as people sang along.

The room was set up with wooden trestle tables, crêpe paper draped over the walls, crisscrossing overhead. Katerina and Luana took seats at one of the back tables with some of their other cousins. It was just dark enough in the room to adequately conceal their box of cheap wine – the jugs of beer on their table, which were sold at the function, had been bought for them discreetly by some kind drunk uncle.

A paper cup full of wine was plonked down in front of them, and they were urged to scull it back, which Luana happily obliged. She alternated between the two beverages – 'To slow down my drinking,' she assured them all – and was onto her third cup by the time Katerina started her first. The wine was sickly sweet; she could barely take another sip.

The floor was flooded with dancers, gyrating in pairs, seducing their partners, the men flapping their legs as the women swayed their hips. Boyfriends, husbands, other women's husbands invited into their personal spaces, gravitating towards each other like magnets.

Luana dragged one of their cousins onto the dance floor and they moved to the sounds of Engelbert Humperdinck. Lip-syncing to 'Spanish Eyes', she flirted with him inappropriately, her eyelids batting.

Katerina rubbed her belly, relieved it was concealed. She was grateful for the cups, jugs, and wine box, which helped to keep her secret, especially as Rahui marched past their table, patrolling the hall. His hands locked behind him, clutching paper and pen, eyes wide open and looking for trouble.

'Kia orana, niece.'

'Hello, Uncle.' Katerina's cheeks reddened as he eyed up the now empty jugs and glasses and his nieces and nephews, giving them a curt nod before moving on. The wine box was stuffed under the table.

Luana returned, her face now flushed from the rampant dancing, her partner, their cousin, following her back.

'Dance with me, cuz.'

'Nah,' said Katerina, gesturing towards their cousin, 'you show me up. I can't compete.'

Luana nodded towards the table of boys across the hall. 'If you don't come and dance with me, cuz, not my fault what happens.'

Katerina followed her gaze and noticed Anaru, flanked by his rugby mates. He'd told her he'd be coming, said he'd be bringing his team with him. He had his back to her so she flicked her head at his mates, who nudged him, forcing him to look up from his beer. His smile still made her heart skip beats. She scanned the room for her mother.

'You going over?' Luana asked, checking out the talent at his table. She recognised most of them, many from school, but there was the odd one she didn't know.

'He can come to me.'

'Nice,' said Luana. 'Play hard to get.' She batted her eyelashes at the boy beside Anaru, who grinned back, flipping his head at her. She looked away and then back at him, her stare even more intense. Katerina was entertained. 'Okay,' said Luana, 'see you.' She excused herself from the table, fleeing the hall, the boy from the other table in pursuit.

Katerina was watching the dancers when she heard the vacant seat beside her scrape against the floor. She recognised

Anaru's scent and felt dizzy. Nausea travelled up her spine and sat in her throat, stifling her voice, blocking words from forming. She turned to him and he smiled, his eyes unblinking, trancelike.

'You're late. I thought you weren't coming.'

'I had to wait for Lu. You know what she's like.'

'She's a character, your cousin.'

He poured himself a beer from the replenished jug, offering her a drink. She blocked the top of her cup with her hand and watched him scull his beer and pour himself another.

'How long do these things last?' He gestured towards the hall, the people on the dance floor, the band on the stage, the rotating mirror ball.

'Till midnight,' she said. 'Then we clean up.' She could feel her mother watching from the opposite side of the hall, her eyes darting between the dance floor and back to her daughter and the boy sitting beside her. 'You know, the usual story' – she gestured towards her mother – 'with the slave driver.' She started to laugh.

'Don't say that about your mum.'

She cringed at his thoughtfulness.

He leaned in towards her and whispered in her ear. 'Let's go outside.'

She suddenly felt exhausted. 'I can't.'

'Why not?'

'My mum.'

'Just for—'

'No.'

The band started playing ABBA, the island rhythm giving the pop song a Polynesian twist. People began to fill the dance floor, shuffling with a mix of disco and island dance moves.

'Kia orana, Katerina.' Eugene hovered beside her.

'Eugene,' she said, relieved. 'Here, sit down.' She shuffled over to let him pull up a chair. The cousins at the table shifted awkwardly along. 'Drink?' she asked, nodding at Anaru.

Anaru poured him a beer. Katerina watched Eugene tap the cup a few times before finally taking a sip.

Eugene scanned the room, his eyes roving over the hall from the stage to the dance floor. In another corner, a clique of girls from school could be seen cackling amongst themselves. Katerina watched him take another sip.

'Why don't you ask her to dance? Go on,' said Katerina. Intuitively she knew which girl he was interested in. She nudged him in the arm, then felt bad when the blush in his cheeks spread to the tips of his ears. She sensed his hesitation, watched as he shifted awkwardly, struggling to muster up the courage to walk over. Katerina ignored her cousins at the table, who were failing to disguise their mirth. 'Do it,' she urged him.

Eugene rose from his seat and moved tentatively towards the girl. It surprised Katerina that his gangly legs weren't tripping him up. He crossed the dance floor, weaving in and out of the pairs of gyrating dancers, and hovered over the girl. Katerina's heart raced for him. She knew Anaru was watching her, could tell he was frustrated that she was giving Eugene more attention. But it mattered nothing.

'Hello, Betty.' Eugene stared down at the crown of the girl's head. The 'ei katu she was wearing eclipsed her face completely. Katerina saw his growing unease as Betty refused to acknowledge him.

'Hello, Betty.' He said it louder this time, then cleared his throat and waited for more words to rise. 'H-hello, Betty. Would you like to dance?'

The cackling from the table was audible to Katerina now and when Betty finally turned in her seat to acknowledge him, it sent a knowing shiver down her spine.

'Pardon?' said Betty.

The other girls at the table struggled to contain themselves.

'W-would – would you like to dance, Betty?' Eugene managed to compose himself, back stiffening. A Freddy Fender cover about falling teardrops serenaded the room.

'Aw, Eugene,' she said, 'sorry, I can't dance with you tonight.' She paused and shared a pitying look with him. 'I got a sore leg, see?' She rubbed her leg as if to relieve it of pain. 'I can't dance tonight, Eugene. My doctor told me to keep off it.'

The girls at the table erupted with laughter as Eugene started the long journey back to his seat.

Suddenly, Katerina's face was beaming in front of him. Eugene avoided meeting her eye.

'Dance, Eugene?'

The girls at the table side-eyed Katerina as she grabbed Eugene's hand and led him to the dance floor. The band started another song with a lively tempo. They weaved through the dancers, who opened up around them, and the misery Katerina felt for Eugene lifted as she witnessed the music moving him. His legs bent at the knees, his arms wide and waving, he invited her into his space. Katerina responded, hips and hands beckoning, and as the beat increased, the space between them closed.

The other dancers stopped to observe them, their excited cheers growing more urgent. Eugene slid across the floor towards Katerina, her hips gently grazing his groin. They spun with the music, the beat suspending them, beads of sweat settling on their foreheads. Katerina swung her hips incessantly, her head in a frenzy and spinning with thoughts.

She thought about her baby. She wasn't concerned about what people thought, but facing her mother made her anxious. The need to own up to her reality, confess the truth, was fast coming up. She knew she couldn't do it alone.

The music stopped and the crowd cheered as she and Eugene came to a sudden halt, breathless. Eugene moved in to kiss her and she let him, turning her head to the side, watching Betty and her cohorts seething at their table.

Eugene escorted her back to their table, beaming all the way as people patted him on the back. Anaru was gone. She looked over at his empty table, then checked her wristwatch. It was just after eleven. She needed some fresh air.

Outside, Katerina breathed deeply. The air was cool and stable, the sky clear, the stars bright. The music from the hall leaked into the street. Everything was calming. She moved to the side of the building, where she could have some privacy. She lit up a smoke and inhaled, and was taking in the peace, when she heard muffled yelps from the open field. She looked for the source – perhaps a dog from the neighbourhood.

There were no lights on the field and the hill behind it was covered with pine trees, which isolated it from the houses nearby. The yelps had turned into grunts when she finally saw signs of movement. As her eyes adjusted to the dark, she caught a glimpse in the moonlight of two tangled bodies. She recognised the black dress, now hiked up to Luana's waist, her bare legs wrapped around the hips of the boy on top of her, whose naked buttocks rose and fell with each thrust.

Katerina watched the pair as they rose and fell into a rhythm, the music from the hall drowning out Luana's soft moans, the boy's urgent grunts. Katerina listened, feeling the same yearning in herself, the pressing need for a touch.

'*Psssh.*'

Katerina turned round. Fetu grinned when he saw what she was looking at.

'You like that?' he asked. The glint in his eye embarrassed Katerina. Feeling exposed, she quickly stubbed out the smoke and straightened up. She smoothed down the sides of her dress, her hands gently roaming over her belly.

His breath on her face soothed her as the space between them closed. He pressed his chest against hers, held her, swaying now to the slow gentle beats of the waltz that was playing. Fetu sang along with the band, taking her hand, pulling her into the shadow. She slipped into his arms, her head resting on his shoulder. Their bodies moved to the song, his breath brushing the nape of her neck.

'You're late,' she said.

'I'm here now.'

'I could've left with someone else.'

'You wouldn't.'

'I could've.'

'You wouldn't.'

He pulled her in and pressed his lips against hers. Ran his hand over her, his fingers brushing her cleavage, tiptoeing down the front of her dress like creeping willow, settling on her growing bump. They danced into the second verse.

'Iosefa?'

'Too churchy.'

'That's my father's name.'

Katerina rolled her eyes. 'Juliet,' she said. 'From *Romeo and Juliet*.'

'We not Palagi. Why you want a Palagi name?' Fetu

grinned. 'And that's a girl's name.' He gently rubbed her stomach again. 'I think our baby's a boy. An All Black.'

He watched Katerina's face light up. 'I don't mind if it's a boy or a girl,' she said, 'as long as we're a family.'

Luana and her boy let out one final grunt. Katerina turned in time to see the boy pull on his pants.

Fetu was still holding Katerina. 'When will you tell your mum?'

'Soon,' she said, not overly confident.

'I will come.'

'No.'

'Yes,' he insisted. 'I want to ask her if I can marry you.'

Katerina felt a flutter in her stomach. She imagined it was their baby. 'How do you know I'll say yes?' she teased.

Luana and the boy hurried past them, the boy making his way down the street, tucking in his shirt. Katerina pulled away from Fetu.

'Hey, cuz,' said Luana, eyeballing Fetu, turning her back on him to acknowledge Katerina. 'You all right? You coming?'

Katerina shook her head.

'Sure, cuz?' Katerina nodded. Reassured, Luana turned to walk back to the hall, grass clippings caught in her hair and dress.

'You want to?' Fetu hadn't taken his eyes off her. She could sense it.

'What?'

'Be a family?'

Katerina remembered her peg family, their imaginary lives. Then she watched Fetu get into his taxi before she rejoined her cousins in the hall.

*

For my daughter, her hair has always been a source of pride. I admit it is beautiful. The long, thick locks are black as coal, smooth like the coconut flesh. Sometimes I imagined seeing my own image in the shine of her hair, like a mirror from one of her silly fairy tales. *Mirror, mirror on the wall. Who's the fairest one of all?* She loved that story.

As she grew, I would see the way the other girls looked at her. The sly stares, the whispering behind cupped hands. They were persistent with their secret taunts, the made-up stories, the name-calling. When she passed them in the street, with those legs of hers that wanted to run, her seeming dismissiveness only heightened their jealousy. They hated her, those girls, and at the same time they wanted to be her. But she never had time for them.

I noticed too the way the boys would stare at her, and the men, grown men – some as old as the father she never knew. They smiled her way when she passed them in the street, their eyes roaming over her like rubberneckers at a car wreck. She learned the strength in a coy look, a secret gaze, a confidential smile.

So when I overheard her and her boyfriend at the dance, it didn't surprise me that she believed in fairy tales. I had hoped it wouldn't come to this.

Sunday, 4 July

Standing behind the pulpit, Rahui clears his throat, an amplified cough that bounces off the concrete walls. Father O'Shea's gaze settles on the back of the room at the large wooden doors open to the narthex. Being a Raro Mass, the choir pit above is vacant. He stares into it, full of apprehension.

'In today's sermon,' Rahui begins, meeting the eyes of his relatives. He speaks in English, as encouraged by Father, to lure in younger churchgoers, make it more inclusive. 'I want to talk about temptations.' The relatives shift uncomfortably. 'Drinking,' he says, 'is the way of the Devil.'

A low rumble of murmurs rises from the pews. Father O'Shea frowns from his seat in the chancel. It isn't uncommon to indulge in a tipple with members of his parish, Rahui included. He has taught them Irish folk songs, learning their songs from the islands in return. It's how he remembers the language – the hard and soft vowels, the limited consonants in the alphabet. They discover commonalities, minimise their differences. It's how his congregation knows they can trust him.

'Some people,' says Rahui, eyeballing certain relatives, 'are hypocrites.'

Father O'Shea's focus is still on the narthex, the faces of his congregation like smudged fingerprints.

'They call themselves good Christians when they're not.' Rahui pauses to let his words sink in. 'They go to their jobs – those who have jobs.' A united gasp near the back of the church. 'They do their work to make some money so they can feed their families and pay their bills. They put a roof over the family, and that's all good.'

Father O'Shea starts shuffling in his seat. The sermon is a ten-minute slot and the church is uninsulated with limited heating.

'Some people work at Todd's,' says Rahui, acknowledging those workers, of which there are a few. 'Some people catch a train into the city.' He nods to the mamas and aunties and older girl cousins who make those journeys to their cleaning jobs. 'Some people, like me, work at the freezing works, killing lambs and boning pigs and making sausage meat like salami and luncheon.'

Katerina's daydreams about disappearing into confessional booths start to feel more urgent.

'Your family can eat sausages or even steak if it's a pay week and your boss is in a kind mood. He might let you have some meat for cheap because he knows you have a big family and it makes him feel like a good person inside. Like a Christian, even though he doesn't go to church.'

He trips over his wife's eyeroll, pausing for a second before finding his voice again.

'Last week I brought home for my family a box of meat from work.'

Father O'Shea focuses long enough to notice the dropped jaws in front of him.

'A kilo of mince – *a whole kilo*. A slab of rump steak – *a slab*. A hundred sausages – *a hundred*. And luncheon, for my children.' Katerina cringes for Moana and Tere in the pew in front of her. 'And you know what else we got?'

The whole congregation sits in stunned silence.

'Hotdogs,' he says. 'The kind you get at the races. On a stick.'

Beside her, Katerina's other cousins stifle their laughs, their cheeks bulging. She holds her belly to comfort herself.

'And that's what I'm talking about,' he says, seeming to come to the point of his sermon. 'Gambling.' Father O'Shea breathes out slowly. 'It's the way of the Devil.'

The aunties and uncles look at each other sideways. It takes all the will of the Holy Spirit not to shake their heads.

'You know' – Rahui leans into the pulpit, making intense eye contact with those in the first row – the children – 'gambling is a sin.'

'I thought you were talking about drinking,' someone calls out. Only the youngest children in the front row, who are scraping old gum from under their seats and eating it, look unperturbed.

'They go to work during the week,' says Rahui, 'on the Mondays to the Fridays—'

'You told us this already.'

'And they buy the nice food for their family. Last week, I brought home some steak and luncheon for my daughters' lunches to take to school.'

There is a collective sigh.

'But then come the weekend, they drink the beer.'

'Who? Your daughters?'

'What about the gambling?'

Father O'Shea stares blankly into the nave.

'They drink the beer and the wine and the spirits.' Rahui pauses, considering. 'But not the Holy Spirit that we come to visit on Sunday, no.' Katerina slumps in her seat. Terepai stares into the giant crucifix on the wall behind her brother. 'They drink the whiskey spirit.' Father O'Shea can feel the flush in his cheeks. 'They drink the bourbon spirit. They drink the vodka spirit. They drink every spirit but the spirit of the Holy Spirit.'

Rahui raises his fist as he laments the virtues of the Holy Spirit.

'Last night, I went to the dance at the community hall. And when I was there, I saw many others in this church today who were there also.' He stares accusingly into the faces of the congregation, sweeping the pews.

'It was a church social!'

Rahui ignores the interjection, waving his fist. 'What I saw was evil. People drinking and carrying on like it's not a sin to drink your troubles away. That's what I saw – people drinking their troubles away like there's no church in the morning.' He breathes in slowly, judgementally. 'But there is church in the morning,' he says, glaring at those relatives he saw the night before, 'and here we all are. Acting like good Christians. Acting like good Christians. *Acting*.'

People start to moan more audibly. Katerina and Terepai's chins fall.

'But are we?' comes Rahui's clincher.

'What? Acting?'

'Are we good Christians?' He pauses again to let people take in his words and then he turns and nods at Father O'Shea. 'This is the Word of God,' he says.

'Thanks be to God,' comes the stilted response.

Monday, 5 July

I am tired. Life has tired me. My eyes this day are heavy with stress. I was woken in the morning in that time between night and day, when the spirits of our ancestors whisper in our dreams. The voices outside my window are not as comforting. At first, I don't recognise my neighbours next door, their words as sharp and direct as the strangers they are speaking to. I press my ear against the glass, careful not to disturb the curtains, covert and undetected.

'Why are you here? It's five in the morning.'

I imagine my neighbours' distress, knowing in their panic who would visit them at this hour, their worries only heightening once they'd opened the door. Even unexpected relatives wouldn't call at this time.

'My family is sleeping. Who told you to come here?'

If I pull the curtains apart just slightly, peek between the drapes at a certain angle, I can see who's on the front doorstep. The sky is black despite the morning hour, but I can see the boy's taxi parked up in the driveway. I watch his empty car, knowing he is inside the house, knowing he's the one they're searching for. In the porch light I can see the two policemen. I pull the curtains open a fraction more, in time to watch the boy's aunty go back into the house, his uncle guarding the door.

Katerina is still asleep. She will need her rest, and not only for the baby growing inside her – the next few days will not be easy. She will act as if she hates me, become more morose and withdrawn. But she will understand, in time, know that I did it for her and my grandchild. I prayed long and hard for the guidance to come through, to know for sure the right thing to do. I didn't come to the decision lightly.

Once he's deported, my daughter, I expect, will never see him again. He will be free to live his life, freeing my daughter to live her life too. No tearful goodbyes, no empty promises to break. I spared her from that. And from being alone. I won't allow it. She has me and her child, and the rest of her family. That is all she needs. I have saved her from a life of unnecessary heartbreak.

*

In the evening, Katerina waits for Fetu. That was their plan, to finally tell her mother. She hasn't heard from him since the night before, but she's not worried.

'Seven,' he'd said. 'I will come to your house at seven.' She watched him creep out of her bedroom window. The sky was black and she could hear the TV in the sitting room, Telethon's final total blaring through the speakers as the studio audience cheered.

She breathes deeply, feeling grateful for the small things. Her mother has been quieter than usual and Katerina welcomes the peace. Soon, everything will be right. She plays with her wristwatch, counting down the minutes.

Acknowledgements

Some of the stories in *Beats of the Paʻu* have appeared in the following publications, and I thank their editors: *adda, Turbine | Kapohau, Sport 46, Takahe, Middle Distance: Long Stories of Aotearoa New Zealand* and *A Game of Two Halves: The Best of Sport 2005–2019*. RNZ National played readings of early drafts of 'The Promotion', 'Love Rules for Island Girls' and 'Love Rules for Island Boys'. The latter stories were inspired by Junot Diaz's 'How to Date a Brown Girl (black girl, white girl, or halfie)'. 'Bluey' was shortlisted for the 2019 Commonwealth Writers Short Story Prize.

It's impossible to thank Te Herenga Waka University Press without acknowledging each individual. THW is the epitome of team, and every staff member is dedicated to supporting each of their authors in helping them to bring their books into the world. So to Fergus Barrowman, Craig Gamble, Ashleigh Young, Kyleigh Hodgson, Jasmine Sargent, Kirsten McDougall and Tayi Tibble: thanks for your support and for bringing my book into the world!

I wrote the first draft of the collection at the International Institute of Modern Letters in 2017. Special thanks goes to IIML MA course convenor and supervisor the ever-brilliant Emily Perkins, for all the advice and support you've given me; and to my classmates from that workshop and writing group—Anthony Lapwood, Antonia Bale, Clare Moleta, Frank Sinclair, Kirsten Griffiths, Lynne Robertson, Mia Gaudin, Nicole Colmar and Sharon Lam—for your continued insights and friendship. Also to Sue Orr and Victor Rodger for early feedback on my manuscript during that year.

I held my first writing residency in the summer of 2018 at the University Bookshop in Dunedin, in association with the Robert Lord Cottage Trust, where I continued to work on *Beats* immediately after the MA. Thank you also to the New York Street residency in Martinborough.

Many thanks to management and my colleagues at Hansard and the Office of the Clerk for your ongoing support and flexibility, especially during the MA year, an election year.

Special thanks to talented friend, artist and writer Kirsten Griffiths for the cover art of the house I grew up in. And to Sean Chen, whose stunning painting 'Parliament Buildings' from the Parliamentary Collection inspired the cover. And to Ebony Lamb for my author photo.

And to the community I grew up in—the Cook Islands Catholic community in Porirua—and the friends, neighbours and extended family I grew up with. The main setting of these stories comes from a time and a place that feels worlds away from today's reality, but while the stories and characters in this collection are fiction, the heart in this book is real.

And, finally, to my parents, Ngametua and Noo Stephen, with the greatest love, for everything.